MW01103937

THE FARTHER SHORE

Also by Rob Davidson

Field Observations: Stories

The Master and the Dean: The Literary Criticism of Henry James and William Dean Howells

THE FARTHER SHORE

ROB DAVIDSON

BEAR STAR PRESS

Printed in the United States of America

5 4 3 2 1

Bear Star Press
185 Hollow Oak Drive
Cohasset, California 95978
www.bearstarpress.com

Book & cover design by Beth Spencer
Author photograph by Linda Rogers
Cover art: *Dharma Vessel* by Adam Shaw
www.adamshawstudio.com

ISBN: 978-0-9793745-9-3
Library of Congress Control Number: 2011938990

ACKNOWLEDGMENTS

Thanks first to my wife, Linda. And to my children, who inspire me every day.

Thanks to the Woodstock Guild and the Byrdcliffe Artist Colony, where some of this book was written. Thanks to the College of Humanities and Fine Arts and the Department of English at California State University, Chico, and to the California State University Research Foundation for their collective support of my creative endeavors. Finally, thanks to the friends and colleagues who read and critiqued these stories, helping to improve them.

I would also like to express gratitude to the editors of the following publications, in which several of these stories originally appeared: "First Position" and "Terminations" in *REAL: Regarding Arts & Letters*; "Tell Me Where You Are" in *New Delta Review*; and "The Student" in *The Quercus Review*. "Criminals," first published in *ZYZZYVA*, won the 2009 Camber Press Fiction award, judged by Ron Carlson. "My Favorite Disaster" first appeared in *The Normal School*; reprinted by permission of *The Normal School*, © 2010 by Rob Davidson.

A few phrases from the "Preface to *The Ambassadors*," by Henry James, have been lovingly borrowed in "Criminals."

"The Student" is for Henry Hughes.

The quotation from the Dhammapada is taken from *Dhammapada: The Sayings of the Buddha*, trans. Thomas Byrom (Boston: Shambhala, 1993).

for Peter

CONTENTS

Wanting nothing
With all your heart
Stop the stream.

When the world dissolves
Everything becomes clear.

Go beyond
This way or that way,
To the farther shore
Where the world dissolves
And everything becomes clear.

Beyond this shore
And the farther shore,
Beyond the beyond,
Where there is no beginning,
No end.

Without fear, go.

—The Dhammapada

FIRST POSITION

My name is Adam Penn. I'm a college graduate, with a BA in music history, thank you, and a musician, most recently the veteran of a half-hearted attempt at breaking into the open mic scene. Fuck and alas, people! Minneapolis does not lack for wry, observant lyricists with mediocre guitar skills. You have to be talented to succeed here, and it helps to be pushy. I'm neither. Ergo the day job. Data entry, in this case. And, please, don't underestimate: it is, quite literally, beyond boring. Soporific is the word. Somnolent. Though I assure you that, for matters of job security, I don't even think about sitting down to work without a twenty-ounce double Americano and fat wad of nicotine gum. (Trying to quit, not quite there, thanks for asking.) But if what you want is complete anonymity coupled with an utter sense of futility, then Compton Consulting is the place for you.

Now, the job does offer one perk. You can listen to a personal radio while you type. I like to stroll through the room after we get a new batch of drones, scanning musical tastes. Mostly it's crap: rap-metal, Top 40, country singers who wear hats. But there's one girl, Ros, she's into vintage Goth: Bauhaus, early Cure, Nick Cave. That's listenable in my book, so I've singled her out. I chat her up at smoke breaks on the street corner, or at the bus stop after work. Ros has a lean, angular face and long arms. A dozen black rubber bracelets encircle her wrist. Her sallow skin suggests she never gets out. That she may not eat right. That there is perhaps something the matter.

So sexy.

Today it is sunny and warm for September. A hint of Indian summer. Ros has agreed to join me for a drink after work. We sit at the north end of Nicollet Mall, on the edge of a little plaza. Across the street from us is a man-made pond with a fountain—the outdoor court of WCCO, a local TV station. A Hmong guy hawks hot dogs from a cart. Ros sips a Bloody Mary. I'm drinking stout. We talk about her stuff: UFOs, tarot cards, celestial arrangements. She picks her nose and wipes it on the tablecloth.

When drones get together, we don't tell each other who we really are. We tell each other who we want to be. I've met actresses, poets, an inventor, and one guy who claimed to have held a professorship in physics at Stanford in the sixties. Ros says she dropped out of college a year ago. Just sort of fell off the rails. She wants to model, but can't work up the initiative. In the mean time, she's thinking about becoming a magician.

"I'm one-eighth gypsy," she says. "My great-grandmother traveled all over Poland, Romania, Hungary. It's in my blood."

"You don't look like a Romany."

"Well, Great-Grams emigrated to Rhode Island. From there, it's all WASP. But one-eighth is enough, let me tell you. It fuels my blood."

"I like the way you say that."

"I go wherever my spirit drags me." She smiles. "What about you?"

I tell Ros I'm a musician. I don't see the need to append the modifier "failed" at this time. "I'm between gigs. I'll be quitting Compton within a week, maybe ten days. I've got a demo out at a couple of labels. It's looking good. Real good."

"You should cut your own CD," Ros says. She lights one of my cigarettes and leaves it dangling from the corner of her mouth, suggestively. "I knew a guy who did that in Madison. Left copies at coffee shops and bars. I wrote the liner notes. It was fun."

"But did he make money?"

She gives me a look like I'm from another planet.

"Cheers," I say, and drink.

"I saw you reading a big, thick book at lunch."

I nod. "*Stone Alone*. Bill Wyman's book. He claims he slept with something like four hundred girls in 1968."

"Yeah, and they were all fourteen," Ros says, laughing. "I don't read anything over two hundred pages, myself. I can't maintain the interest level."

"It's that gypsy blood."

"Yeah, maybe." She lifts her chin and runs her tongue across her lips. "Want me to read your palm?"

I smile and extend my hand across the table to her. She traces her fingertips lightly across my palm. Her nails are chewed down to the nubs.

"What do you see?"

She gently presses the tip of her index finger into the center of my hand. "You're thinking about asking me out somewhere. Dinner. A show or something."

"Hey, you're good."

She sits back in her chair. She takes a strand of blue-black hair into the corner of her mouth and slowly chews on it.

"And what do you say when I ask?"

"You have to ask," she says. She grinds her cigarette into the ashtray. "Gypsies don't predict results. We just see possibilities."

So I ask her.

This is how it starts.

Andy Hartley comes over to my house one spring afternoon to watch the four o'clock movie on KDLH, hosted by Jack McKenna. Andy and I are fourth graders at Washburn Elementary in Duluth, Minnesota. The movie that day is *A Hard Day's Night*. I've never seen it, never even heard of the Beatles. Suddenly four guys in tight suits are running down the street, chased by hundreds of screaming teenage girls. A little frightening (we were ten), but cool to be so adored. Then a twelve-string guitar chord chimes and the title track begins. For the next two hours Andy and I are entranced by everything we see and hear: the bushy hair, the charming accents, the jokes we don't understand. Then there's the music. During "Can't Buy Me Love" we pogo on the couch in my mother's basement, shouting with glee as the Beatles cavort aimlessly in an empty field at double speed.

It is the greatest film I have ever seen. It is the greatest music I have ever heard. Still.

At a downtown bar we eat oysters on the half shell and drink Campari. I love a woman who will consume raw shellfish. Ros says sushi is her favorite finger food. Under the table, I slide a hand over her knee. She gives me an encouraging nod. I haven't felt this good all year.

It's her idea to skip dinner. "Who needs dinner?" she says. "The food will just kill my buzz." I have nothing against a good buzz on an empty stomach. I take her out into the street. We wend our way between the glittering towers of Minneapolis, those fingers of jade and steel and light. On the Hennepin Avenue Bridge, we walk out over the Mississippi, the water below us a broad, silky ribbon.

"When the Replacements signed to Warner Brothers," I say, "they didn't want the corporate bigwigs buying out their early work. So, they traipsed into the office of Twin Tone Records, up on Nicollet Avenue, and they sweet-talked the secretary into letting them take all of the masters for their first four records. And they came right here, to this bridge, and they threw the tapes into the river."

Ros turns to look at me, then down to the river, then bursts out laughing. "That's brilliant!" She rubs her hands along the metal railing, then forms a fist and bangs it. It rings with a dull, hollow sound. "Didn't John Berryman jump into this river?"

"Yeah. I think he leapt from the Washington Avenue Bridge, over near the U."

"I read that he was smiling as he fell."

"He probably gave a little wave. What difference does it make? He's dead."

She turns to face me. "Did you ever think about killing yourself?"

"No," I say. "I don't believe in an afterlife. All the glory and the pain is right here, today. You just have to live this life."

"Yeah, but why?"

"Do you mean, like, is there a Cosmic Theory for Everything?" I turn to look at the enormous Grain Belt beer sign on the east bank of the river. Its neon reds and greens look sort of holy, in a shopping-mall, Christmassy kind of way. "Do you have to have a reason to live? Can't you just, I don't know, do it?"

"Maybe," she says. She puts her feet up on the lowest rung of the pedestrian guardrail and steps up. "But it's like, if you kill yourself, you must have a reason. So, if you don't kill yourself, don't you need a reason not to?"

"Wait. I think you just used a double negative."

"I'm serious," she says. She steps up to the middle rung of the railing. Her thighs press against the top rail. Bending at the waist, she leans forward, over the river. Her skirt flutters in the breeze—white polka dots on navy, like a handful of stars dancing just out of arm's reach. It's a pretty sight, but I'm worried about those black carpenter's boots she wears. If she slips on the rail, she'll pull a Berryman. I move a step closer.

"Okay, you want to know what I live for? Music. For writing and playing and listening to music."

"Good," she says. "That's good." She's quiet for a moment, then asks, "What's your reason to die?"

I laugh as I light a cigarette. "Who are you, Jim Morrison and shit?"

"You only need one reason. If it's good enough, you'll do it." She throws her hands back, like a bird spreading its wings. Her hair bounces gently in the breeze.

I put a hand on her waist. "Get down from the railing."

"Do I make you nervous?" she asks, smiling coyly over her shoulder. In a moment, she's down and I move to her, wrap my arms around her, pull her close. I give her a puzzled look.

"Do a lot of gypsies kill themselves?" I ask.

"No, I don't think so. Not any more than average, I would say."

"Well, that's good."

"And, anyway, you don't have to worry because I have a very good reason for staying alive."

"Let's have it."

"I want to break all ten commandments before I die." A sly smile forms in one corner of her mouth. She draws a fingertip lightly under my chin. "I've only got one more to go."

"Hold on a minute," I say, pulling back playfully.

She shakes her head slowly, then leans forward and whispers into my ear, "I've already killed someone." She gives me a quick kiss on the lips, then slips out of my arms. She walks with a girlish skip, hands dancing at her sides. A vision luminous, smooth, unidentifiable.

A song is a way of gathering in the loose bits and fragments of your life and making something beautiful out of it. It's a little corner of your existence that you compress, distill, mold and reshape until the melody fits the words. A song can lift you up, take you out of your banal existence and put you somewhere, if only for a few minutes, better than where you are right now. But you have to believe in the song. You have to believe that you can sing it, that the song is yours to sing. What it is, is a matter of faith.

On the bus back to Uptown, I explain my Theory of Musical Relativity: Every conceivable human emotion has been expressed in a song. All you have to do is search hard enough and you'll find it—that voice for what you feel.

"So everybody should just do covers? Is that what you're saying?"

"Not at all. You have to write your own stuff. The particular embodying the universal, and all that. Look at Joni Mitchell."

"I don't listen to her," Ros says. She's studying the passengers on the bus. "You talk a lot about other people's music. What are your songs like?"

"My stuff?" I lean back, looking out the window, over my shoulder. "Sort of new folk meets cowpunk. It's all acoustic. Singer-songwriter stuff."

"Will you play me some?"

"Yeah, okay. Maybe," I say, shifting my haunches.

"What, don't you have any songs?"

"I got songs," I say, hastily. "It's just—I haven't been playing out much recently. Fingers are a little stiff, you know."

Ros gives me a quick, gentle smile. I've never felt more transparent. "Well, I want to hear you." She leans forward and brushes the bangs from my eyes. "The boy with the briar patch hair," she says, with a little laugh.

We get off at West 26th Street, a few blocks shy of Calhoun Square. I'm in the mood to walk. I'm thinking of a wee stroll around Lake of the Isles 'neath verdant boughs, the indigo sky spattered with early stars, etc. We cross at the corner and Ros stops before the display window of the Condom Kingdom. Camouflage, double-size, edible. A hand-written sign in one corner of the window announces, "We Have Dental Dams!" Ros asks if I have a flavor preference.

"Strawberry," I say. "No, mango."

"They've got both!"

"Do they have a dressing room?"

"Can you try before you buy?"

"There should really be a recycling program."

"Why recycle? Go edible!"

I take her hand. A swarm of traffic pours behind us like a song.

Later, in my small room, we drink tequila by candlelight and listen to Beth Orton. I burn a stick of my favorite incense, sandalwood. Eventually, Ros asks me to play her some songs. I drink a quick shot. The stereo goes off and I take out my battered acoustic, a cheap Korean import covered in stickers and taped-on photos of freak show people, strange-looking animals, a burning monk. It looks cool, but the guitar is a big piece of shit. The action is too high and the intonation is all off. Everything above the tenth fret is out of tune. Not that it matters. I can't solo to save my life, and my songs are all in the first position. They almost all start in G because I can't really sing in any other key.

I sing her one song about a guy who falls in love with a department store mannequin, then another about a guy who falls in love with a dinosaur. (Well, the fossilized remains of a dinosaur, as displayed at a museum.) My third song is about the difficulties of recycling. As I sing, Ros walks around my room, inspecting the messy stacks of CDs and the concert posters taped to the wall—Run Westy Run, Hüsker Dü, and my patron saint, Jonathan Richman. She pauses before the one nice thing I own: a gift from the director of my undergraduate honors thesis, a framed print of Robert Fludd's Celestial Monochord. I keep playing my tunes, and she keeps pretending she isn't listening. It's nice that way. I don't want her staring at me like the people in the coffee shops. Laughing when you're not trying to be funny. When I'm done I lay the guitar on the mattress beside me. The windows are open and the blinds are up. The pale glow of the halogen streetlights washes the walls in soft orange. I'm sure Ros's silence speaks for itself. She kneels before me.

"You don't have to say anything. Honestly."

She places a finger to my lips. It is warm and smells of soap. "Your songs are . . . different. But beautiful, in a funny, back-of-the-drawer kind of way."

"Like a lint ball?"

She smiles. "They're about such odd things. People might like them, if you didn't sound so nervous. You're choking them."

And I tell her: that's why I can't play out. I'm fucking terrified. I tell her how, when I finished school, I cut a demo and hit the open mics. I thought I was ready. But people will say things to you. You can't sing. You can't write. You can't play the guitar. Don't come back, don't call, don't quit your day job. They really say that shit.

"You can't listen to that," she says, quietly. "You can't let it get to you."

I place a hand on her slender forearm, stroke it gently. "Ros, Ros, Ros. I need a room full of you."

She climbs into my lap and our melody begins.

The next morning, Saturday, I treat Ros to breakfast at Jordan's, a little café around the corner from my place. She orders a roll and coffee. Me, I'm ravenous. I order a farmer's plate heaped with hash browns, eggs, a pancake—the works. Ros picks at her roll like a bird. She wears one of my vintage bowling shirts. I ask her which commandment remains to be broken.

"Do you know them?"

"The Ten Commandments? Ooh, it's been a few years. But you've got no killing."

She holds out a hand, one finger extended.

"No adultery. No stealing. No coveting thy neighbor's goods. No lies. Uh, jeez." She holds up a hand, five fingers spread wide. "Okay, help me out here."

She shakes her head dismissively. "No graven images, honor thy parents, never take the name of God in vain, keep the Sabbath, and," she says, leaning forward, "no god before God."

"So, let's see. Adultery? I can't help you with that. Unless you're . . . you aren't married, are you?"

Laughing, Ros shakes her head. "No god but God. I've done everything but worship a god other than God. And it's the first commandment. It's a biggie."

"Is it? That one doesn't seem hard."

"Actually, when you think about it, it's the hardest of the lot." She sips at her coffee, holding the mug between her hands. "You have to have a god to break the first commandment. You have to believe. That's the hard part."

"Okay, so you're not religious," I say. "Don't you have a favorite store?"

"I like Target. It's cheap but actually kind of hip. I bought this skirt there."

"So, here you go: We take the bus out to the Mall of America and we bow down before Camp Snoopy. The mall—it's like a cathedral. Tall walls reaching to the heavens. Skylights beaming down the celestial beneficence. A congregation milling about. Fellowship. The communion of the charge card—each transaction a piece of the holy body. I'll worship with you. I need some blue jeans, anyway."

Ros laughs. "I like that," she says. "You're good for me. But it wouldn't work. I don't really believe in shopping. Not that way."

I wipe my mouth on a napkin. "What do you care so much about religion for, anyway? I mean, aren't they all sort of, you know, equally full of crap?"

She frowns as she runs a fingertip around the lip of her coffee cup. "There has to be something to explain why we're here. Why this world is the way it is."

"Why, is it all that bad?"

She turns her roll around on her plate, first this way, then that. She puts a hand to her forehead and closes her eyes. She sits like that for a long moment—long enough that I'm about to tell her she doesn't have to go there, whatever it is. But then the hand returns to her lap.

"This is not a pretty story, I'm telling you that right up front," she says. And she proceeds to tell me of her circle of friends in high school, who got together to wear black and gob on excessive amounts of eyeliner. They drank, popped pills, smoked whatever they could find . . . SOP for any high school rebel. Enter Candace, the One True Friend. She and Ros did absolutely everything together, fed off one another in a weird way. They pushed things, played around a little. Held hands in public. They necked once at a party, just to get people talking. There might have been some latent sexual stuff there (uh, really?), but it was more about Us versus Them, which these two cultivated like a rare plant.

But it went too far. They started scaring people off, even their Goth buddies. "Not that I have anything against lesbians," Ros says, "or even being one. I just saw how we'd taken this thing, which was sweet and funny for a while, to an extreme. My world had shrunk to one person. I wanted to find an out. And I tried, I really did. But Candace had a way of clinging to you, of sinking her claws in.

"Oh, this girl was a real piece of work. She'd had some eating disorder and was a cutter, to boot. Capital-D dysfunction. Her dad was a bigshot at Norwest Bank, always out of town. Mom pretty much lived at the country club. They owned a mansion on Lake Minnetonka, an acre of beachfront, but Candace lived in the basement, in a little room with blacked-out windows. Candles all over the place. Like a little crypt—with a four-thousand-dollar stereo, that is.

"So, we're in there one night, listening to Love and Rockets or whatever, and screwing around with the Ouija board, when Candace says it's time to play the Marilyn Monroe game. She's got a pile of her mother's sleeping pills and a big bottle of whiskey. She puts a pill on the table, pours a shot, and stares at me. Now, I'm thinking, This is totally freaky. We've done some sick shit, but never anything like this. I figure it's a head game, she's trying to psych me out. So, okay, I swallow a pill and take a shot. Then Candace follows suit. After four rounds, I'm dizzy. My arms feel like lead pipes. I tell her let's stop, but she just laughs. You stop first, she says. So I do. I stop right there. But she keeps popping pills and tossing back the whiskey. I tell her, You win. There's nothing to prove now. But she just keeps laughing. You want me to stop? she says. Then you stop me. Staring me dead in the eyes. She pops another pill, drinks another shot. Does this every minute or two. You don't want me to stop, she says. You want to watch me kill myself. You want me to die. I tell her to knock it off, even try to grab the bottle, but she slaps my hand away. If you want me to live, she keeps saying, you have to stop me."

Ros picks up a spoon and turns it around in her hand, studying it carefully for some time. "After a point, it gets fuzzy, what I can remember. I want to remember that I tried to stop her. I want to remember that I got up, threw her down or something. I want to remember that I tried to save her."

We stare into each other's eyes—hers are a lovely shade of Irish green—and I see she's about to cry. I try to think of something, anything to say. But it's so sad, so far out, that I just have to sit with it first.

"I let her die," she says. "I killed her."

"No, Ros. That's not true. You can't say that."

"Why didn't I do something?" She pushes her plate away. It clacks loudly against a water glass, spilling a little. "Because I hated her, and she knew it, and . . ." Then she's just sort of gone, staring down at the table like it might tell her something, answer all her questions. A moment later, she's weeping.

I help her stand from the table and guide her slender hand as she fumbles with the sleeve of her sweater. And I hold her, right there in the café, in front of all those people. I wrap my arms around her body, pull her close, and let her cry, each tear knocking against the door of my heart, willing it to open an inch more. To stop asking cynical questions of the world. To be raw and unafraid.

In 500 BC, Pythagoras discovered that the musical scale can be expressed as a series of mathematical proportions. This led Pythagoras, who applied mathematics to all phenomena, to believe that the spacing of the celestial bodies represented a kind of cosmic tuning, or harmony—"the music of the spheres," he called it.

Two thousand years later, English Rosicrucian and polymath Robert Fludd composed a theory of mathematical harmony in the universe, represented visually in his drawing of the Celestial Monochord: a one-stringed instrument tied firmly, at one end, to earth, the realm of Man. The other end was tuned by the hand of God. In Fludd's drawing, the sun hangs midway between God and Man—the octave on the divine scale. Fludd's monochord, whose fourteen intervals produce fifteen notes, connected the known material and spiritual worlds in an elegantly structured system corresponding to the musical scale as he understood it. Between Man and God are the four elements (earth, water, air and fire), followed by the seven known planets (the moon, Mercury, Venus, the sun, Mars, Jupiter and Saturn). Beyond Saturn lay the Realm of Fixed Stars, succeeded by the Three Angelic Hierarchies.

Fludd's Monochord, of course, doesn't explain the cosmos—or the musical scale—as we know it today. The moon and the sun aren't planets. We know what lies beyond Saturn. And we have J. S. Bach to thank for dividing the octave into twelve intervals, rather than Fludd's fifteen. But what does any of that matter now? Robert Fludd was a mystic. He sought, devised, and believed in a system of complete harmonic concordance between God and Man, and the universe as he knew it could be expressed in precise mathematical and musical proportion. For Robert Fludd, the universe was a song. And everything was in tune.

After Ros quit Compton—a month ago, now—she picked up something part-time at a knick-knack joint in Dinkytown, where she can talk to undergrads about the Zodiac and read tea leaves. Equally dead-end, but at least it plays to her nature. We see each other a lot. I'm writing songs again and whenever I have a new one I run it by her. Except for one. "The Boy with the Briar Patch Hair." My first love song. Well, love song about human beings. That is, one human loving another sort of thing. But it's not cheesy or plastic or fake. It's good. No, I mean it! It is!

Anyway, about a week ago Ros took a handful of my demo CDs—they were just dust magnets under my bed—and told me she was going to put a little heat under the mother. I sort of told myself to forget about it, but fuck and alas if she didn't leave a message on my machine last night telling me to call in sick and get down to the Scupperhole at noon tomorrow. And to bring my guitar. All day, I've been second guessing myself. If I should go or not. I think I'm going to puke.

The Scupperhole is a long room, narrow and dark with a low ceiling and exposed pipes. The front half, by the windows, has a few tables across from a narrow bar. In the back half, a broad ledge runs at hip level along both walls. If you arrive early you claim a spot on one of those ledges and you don't relinquish it. I know because I've been here a dozen times to see bands. The place reeks of stale cigarette smoke. I walk in, scanning the room for Ros. She sits at the bar, nursing a Bloody Mary. I kiss her, then ask what I'm doing there.

"You're auditioning for a spot. See the guy with the ponytail? That's Nick. He and I sort of go back a bit, but forget about that. Just go and play for him."

"Maybe I should have a drink." I order a Scotch on the rocks. Then make it a double. Jerry Springer is on the television in the corner. Ros and I watch a fat woman in a chair sob while some guy prances around in his underwear, working the crowd.

"Why do people watch that shit?" Ros asks. "It's so humiliating."

"I got no pity for those people," the bartender quips as she rinses glasses in the sink. A silver hoop dangles from her septum and bounces against the top of her lip. "They make their money. Show some tit or throw a chair, you get a fucking bonus. The way I see it, you step on that stage, you're asking for it."

I take a big belt off the Scotch. "I think I should go back to work now."

Ros grabs my hand and squeezes it tight. "This is your work. And you'd better get used to it, because it looks like we might have another audition at the 400 Club on Thursday."

I lift my eyebrows. "'We'?"

Ros raises her glass and we toast. "Oh, and I need more of your demos." Then she sends me on my way, drink in hand. I walk slowly to the back of the club. I place my guitar along the lip of the barren stage—just one lonely stool on a dirty patch of red Berber carpet. The ponytail guy approaches sporting a Jam T-shirt, the one with the mod target.

"Aaron?"

"Adam. Adam Penn."

"Yeah, sorry. I'm Nick." We shake hands. "I heard your demo. It's okay, man. You need somebody who knows how to run a mixing board."

"Uh, thanks."

"I'll be up front, okay? This is just a favor to Ros, who I love dearly. It's true I do have a couple of slots for an opener next month. No promises. But you never know, you might impress me." He frowns when he sees my guitar, then frowns again when he hears that it doesn't have a jack nor do I have an acoustic pickup. "I love all you artistic geniuses with your shitty equipment." He lights a cigarette, then shrugs his shoulders. "I'll mic you through the PA. It's gonna sound like crap, but I just want to know if you can play and sing at the same time. Hop up there."

I settle in on the stool, adjusting my weight and wishing to hell I had new strings on the guitar. The ones I've got are tarnished and will sound dull and flat. Nick places a microphone on a stand inches from the guitar's sound hole. He positions another in front of my face. The track lighting overhead is warm on my neck.

"Don't move too far from either mic, or no one will hear a thing. The volume will go up and down a bit on the first tune while I set the EQ."

"How long should I play?"

"I'll let you know," he says, drawing a finger across his throat. "You do know you're really lucky."

"Dude, totally. I appreciate this."

Nick laughs. "No, I mean about Ros. The way she talks about you."

"She's fond of hyperbole," I say. My fingers fumble at the tuning pegs. In and out of tune. It seems my low E string just won't stay put.

"If you say so. But I've known her since middle school. You're damn lucky, even if you don't know it. She's a true believer." He flicks his cigarette to the floor, then steps on it. "All right," he says, walking back toward the sound board, "let her rip."

The PA hums with static, an emptiness waiting to be filled. I take a sip of Scotch and clear my throat. From her seat at the bar, Ros flashes me a wide grin and an overpronounced thumbs-up. I can't help but laugh. Something feels good right now and I'm not going to wait to hang a label on it. The few heads in the bar turn when I strum the first chord of my new song. I close my eyes and lean forward to sing, the words close on my lips.

TERMINATIONS

There is something wrong with the baby. Mike's pregnant wife, Nicole, calls with the news. "A genetic error in a chromosome," she says, her voice quavering. She's on her cell phone, which means she's in a back room of the law office, or in the parking lot. Out of earshot. Daubing at her tears carefully, Mike knows, so that she won't smudge her make-up. Nicole always wants to look perfect.

The doctors want a second amnio and more tests, she says. They have to go to Sacramento next week, to a women's clinic, where they'll meet with a genetic counselor. "I knew something was wrong," she whispers into the phone. "I told you."

"Hey, now. We're keeping it positive, right?" Mike flips the page on his desk calendar, checking dates. "You sound terrible. Let me come get you. I'll drive you home."

She refuses, says she doesn't want to lose a sick day. He knows it's not just that. With a baby coming, they're counting every penny. He's returned to a full-time schedule at the car lot, cutting back to just two classes at the university. Graduation is now two, maybe three semesters away.

A skinny kid wearing a basketball jersey and ball cap with the brim turned sideways enters the show room. He's grinning, walking with that bounce in his step. An easy kill.

"I've got a fish on the line," Mike says. "Gotta run. I'll call when I can." He whispers a sweet name into the phone before hanging up. Then he struts out onto the floor and shakes the kid's hand. Ross is his name, and he wants to test drive the new Mustang, a red one with a rear spoiler and chrome mags. In the car, Ross immediately throws the seat all the way back, tilts the steering wheel down into his crotch, and cranks up the stereo. Smiling, Mike all but sleepwalks through the test drive.

Back in the show room, they sit at Mike's desk. The credit check is clean, so he starts working the loan. Ross can only put down three percent. Mike quotes him an interest rate, a typical payment. Ross sinks in his chair, eyes narrowing. But Mike is good. He knows how to keep the song and dance going. He asks if Ross has a girlfriend, and does she like cars? Ross nods.

"What's she going to say when you pick her up in that pony tonight?"

"She gonna freak," Ross says, grinning.

"Damn straight," Mike says. "And you blasting your 50 Cent. Now check this out."

They find a monthly payment Ross can live with, an eighty-four-month loan with an obscene APR. The kid will be upside-down on the car for years, if he doesn't default first. There was a time, early in his career, when Mike felt guilty stringing this kind of loan. But around the office they're a grand slam, and he's been on a dry streak. He moves cautiously toward the close, backing off from the extended service plan, the roadside assistance, and all the tie-ins that are "discounted" for buyers who finance through the dealer. This kid is close to the edge, and Mike wants to wrap the deal up. He's worried about Nicole and the baby. He wants to call his wife, to make sure she's all right.

Finally, after a long hour, Ross signs the loan and is sent to someone else's office. Mike walks the paperwork down the hall to Randy, the sales manager. Randy's necktie is loose around the collar, the top button of his dress shirt unfastened. He flips through the loan paperwork quickly, looking for key numbers.

"About time you bagged some fresh meat," Randy says. "Still, that kid was green. I expected more."

"He was starting to cool," Mike says, shrugging his shoulders. "I didn't want to kill the deal."

"See," Randy says, pointing a finger at him, "that's a self-defeating attitude. That's a guy in a slump talking, getting cautious when he should be confident. Confidence sells cars, Mike. Confidence and finesse. Your bigshot professors can't teach you that, because the only thing they ever sold is the textbook they wrote, 'Theories of Business.'" Randy waves a hand, as if shooing a fly. "You want my theory of business? Get in the fucking trenches and learn how to slop mud."

Mike nods as if he's receiving a great teaching. He knows Randy resents him for going back to school to finish his business degree. Mike will be his own boss some day, and it sure as hell won't be cars. Cars depreciate. Real estate doesn't, at least not in California. Mike grew up in Chico. In his lifetime, this little college town in the Sacramento Valley has grown by a third. And the people keep coming, snatching up orchards, filling in wetlands, creeping up into the foothills. They're even building on an old dump. If you can find a patch of dirt to sell, you can make a million bucks. That's Mike's plan.

When Randy is finished, Mike thanks him for the advice. Then he asks for next Thursday off. Randy drops the pile of paperwork into his outbox. "What, is your prof taking you on a field trip? Don't forget your sack lunch."

Mike fakes a laugh. "It's not for school. My wife needs to see a doctor."

"She sick?"

"No," he says, shifting his feet. "She's expecting."

Randy lifts his eyebrows, then stands from his chair and shoots out a hand. "Congrats! I had no idea you guys were trying."

Mike shakes Randy's hand, matching the firmness of the grip. "We weren't. Just got lucky, I guess you'd call it."

"Well, all right, then. You do what you gotta do." As they walk slowly out into the show room, Randy's eyes scan the floor. "When's the due date?"

"May."

"Boy or girl?"

"We're waiting. We want to be surprised."

"Sure you do. Hey, that's great news." He claps Mike on the back. "Way to go, killer."

On Thursday, Mike and Nicole drive to Sacramento. It's early December. Their route south on Highway 99 takes them alongside bare-limbed almond orchards and rice fields covered in standing water. It's an unusually clear day for the Valley: the Coast Range to the west is precisely defined against the brilliant blue sky. To the east, the green foothills of the Sierra Nevada, a few snowy peaks in the distance. Most days, the mountains are fuzzy, obscured by haze and clouds. But on a day like today, he thinks, you see the lines around you quite clearly.

Nicole sits beside him, wearing a black V-neck sweater over a white T-shirt. Her long hair is held back by a lime green band. Sunglasses hide the dark circles beneath her eyes. He reaches across and takes her hand in his.

"I'm not going to look at the ultrasound today," she says. "I can't."

"Okay, I understand." She means in case they must terminate. The ob/gyn has explained that, by the time the second round of test results come in, it will be week twenty-two. In California, it is difficult to find a clinic that will perform an abortion after week twenty-five. They will have a three-week window—if they get bad news.

"I'm dying for a cigarette," she says. She reaches over and turns on the stereo, finds Kate Wolf singing her slow rendition of "Peaceful Easy Feeling," alone at the piano. She sings along in a soft voice, tapping the beat on her knee. "I love this song," she says, "the way she does it. It's so intimate, it's frightening."

He gently squeezes her hand. "I've got some vinyl in the baby's room, if I can find the box. We'll play it tonight."

"It's a storage room," she says, turning her face to the window, "and you'll never find anything in there. It's a total disaster."

The genetic counselor's office is a small, windowless room in the back of the clinic. Sharon, a stout blonde with chubby, angelic cheeks, speaks bluntly, almost with impatience. Not exactly comforting, Mike thinks, if that's what she's trying to be. But Nicole seems alert, sitting forward in her chair.

Sharon explains that their condition is known as a Trisomy 9 mosaicism: there are three copies of the number 9 chromosome instead of the usual two. It's possible that nothing is wrong. Out of twenty-two cell samples from the initial amniocentesis, only one came back as a possible Trisomy 9. Many labs wouldn't even report this result to a patient. It would be recorded as a pseudomosaicism—an aberration that can be accounted for statistically—and essentially ignored. But Sharon isn't comfortable with that diagnosis because of the limited sample. If, after testing two hundred more cells, no further positives result, she will rule the initial result a pseudomosaicism.

"But I must emphasize," Sharon says, tapping a stack of literature with her fingertip, "that once a Trisomy 9 has been identified it can never be completely ruled out. Even if all the tests we do today come back clean, there will always be the possibility that we're dealing with a T-9 baby."

"And if Baby does have it?" Nicole asks.

Sharon speaks for several minutes about the symptoms, which can vary in range and severity. But the list of possibilities is enough to make Mike feel faint: retardation both intrauterine and mental; congenital heart defects; physical abnormalities such as a bulbous nose, short eyelid folds, low-set ears. Problems with the genitals or the kidneys. Liver failure. Early death is a possibility.

"Oh god," Nicole mutters.

The counselor pushes a sheet across the desk, some data for them to consider. They sit forward to examine it. Immediately, Nicole makes a sharp, sucking sound, a primal inhalation. She sits back, covers her face with her hands, and begins to weep.

"What?" Sharon asks. "What is it?"

"It's a boy," Nicole says, waving a hand frantically.

Mike sees the line on the report. Sex: male. He points to it. "We weren't supposed to know."

"Oh, I'm sorry," Sharon says. "I should have blacked that out."

"We told you we didn't want to know!" Nicole says.

Sharon calmly laces her fingers together. "Yes, you did. You told me that." She shakes her head, slowly. "I'm very sorry. That was a professional lapse on my part. I apologize." She moves a folder from one side of her desk to the other. "Most people these days want to know."

"We didn't want to know!" Nicole snaps.

Sharon excuses herself for a moment. Could she bring them anything to drink? Mike asks for a cup of coffee, black. Nicole declines.

They'd planned on a nice dinner out, a French bistro in Old Sacramento, followed by a stroll along the river. But Nicole wants to head home, even though it means hitting the evening rush hour. They don't speak until they've reached Yuba City, forty miles south of Chico.

"If this baby is unhealthy," she says suddenly, "I don't want it. I can't give myself over to an unhealthy baby. I can't live with a deformed child. I know that's horrible to say, but it's the truth."

Mike changes lanes to pass a slow-moving truck. "Let's wait for the tests. We'll know more in ten days."

"But even if the tests are clean, we won't know. It could still be there." A moment later, she adds, "We won't tell anyone. We'll call it a miscarriage."

He takes a deep breath. He's scared, contemplating a decision he doesn't want to make. "Let's not talk like that," he says, finally. "Not yet."

"We have to decide. The tests might clarify things, or they might not. Still, we have to make up our minds."

Ahead, the traffic light changes to yellow. Mike knows he should slow to a stop, but instead he guns it. The light turns red well before he enters the intersection. A car pulls out. Mike swerves, narrowly avoiding a collision. Someone honks.

"Slow down!" Nicole shouts, throwing a hand up to the dash.

"Sorry," he says, downshifting. His heart pounds. "Can we stop somewhere? I need a drink."

Nicole points to an Applebee's on the next corner. Inside, she heads immediately for the restroom. Mike gets a table and orders a Scotch on the rocks. "Make it a double," he instructs, "and a glass of chardonnay for my wife." For the past four months, she's allowed herself the occasional glass of wine. Those months, he reflects, have been rough. From the start, Nicole has had a bad feeling about the pregnancy. Any child not conceived out of choice, she says, not lovingly brought into this world, is a bad omen. Mike disagrees. The baby beat incredible odds—Nicole was on the pill. That has to mean something. Still, she says it doesn't feel right.

Now, Mike wonders if Nicole might be correct. The thought of raising a child, healthy or not, is terrifying. Married for just over a year, in their early thirties, they're house poor, fighting to make it every month. Nicole is secure in her job at the law office, but her salary is modest. She's still paying down her student loans. Mike is impatient to finish his degree, abandoned ten years ago. He was living at home then, sponging off his mother, until she abruptly decided to join Mike's father in Vacaville. This, after the man had walked out on his wife and child—Mike thought all for the better—some five years prior. Suddenly, Mike needed a job and a place to stay; he sure as hell wasn't moving in with his father. His parents picked up right where they'd left off, screaming their complaints at each other's backs. They're still at it to this day.

School fell by the wayside as Mike bounced between dead-end jobs, waiting for some big idea to sprout, for someone to appear and give him a direction, for an opportunity to fall into his lap. None of that happened. He turned thirty and realized he'd become one of those people he used to make fun of, wandering through life. Faking it. Living in a world of might-have-been.

Returning to school was the first step in changing that. He met Nicole in a world lit class, during a breakout session on Achebe's *Things Fall Apart.* In a room of undergrads wearing ripped blue jeans and hooded sweatshirts, she stood out in her skirt and blouse. He'd always liked a classy dresser, a woman with a hint of make-up and perfume. It created a presence, a kind of force. She looked ready for the world, took things on her own terms. Nicole was from Grass Valley, an old mining town up in the mountains, a stone's throw from Lake Tahoe. A great place, as she put it, to leave behind. She'd been married and divorced there, a pretty ugly scene, and had come to Chico to start over. Mike couldn't believe how focused she was, how hard she worked. It was more than impressive: it was inspiring. She graduated with honors in criminal justice and, a few weeks later, landed a good job in a lawyer's office. They were dating a little by then, and he took her out to celebrate, bought her a steak dinner and poured her a glass of wine. Took her dancing. At midnight, he hired a horse-drawn carriage for a tour of Bidwell Park. Creek water burbled between oak and sycamore; a warm June breeze brushed their hair; she held his hand as he named the stars for her. "You're sweet," she said at the end of that night, "stay close." And he did.

The waitress appears with their drinks. Mike scans a menu, thinking he might eat something. But he knows that Nicole will not join him. She is too stressed to eat, and he won't eat before her, alone. He reaches for his drink. Neither of them had planned on kids, at least not yet. They didn't feel ready. But maybe you're never ready for a kid, he thinks. Maybe things happen this way because you have to break the mold to move forward. Until now, until this pregnancy and the possibility that there is a problem, he hasn't doubted Nicole's trust and confidence in him. They've been close in all things. Maybe they still are. But he needs to feel that they're in it together. He needs to feel that they're staying close, not drifting apart. And he isn't sure.

It was Nicole who'd insisted that they not be told the baby's sex. Mike had wanted to know from day one. Why wouldn't you want to know? Shouldn't you be picking out names, planning ahead? He pressed at first, then backed off when he saw that he was upsetting her. And so they've only announced the pregnancy to family and a few close friends. She hardly talks about it, even with him. But it's on her mind: he's watched the bookmark slowly make its way, week after week, through the copy of *What to Expect When You're Expecting* that she keeps on her night stand.

Now he understands that she's been protecting herself, just in case. She's afraid—more than she'll admit. Because if he's learned anything in his first year of marriage it is the delicate art of reading his wife's silences. Those are the deepest parts of her. At first, he mistook Nicole's quiet demeanor for a kind of dignity, or strength: a tough, tight-lipped pose. And it can be that, sometimes. But it's not *only* that. Silence also covers her fear. When she's scared or weak, she retreats inward, closing out the world. Talking to her then is about as easy as prying a clam open with a credit card.

He learned all this the hard way. It took a few one-sided arguments, with him finally yelling at the wall in the garage, alone, before he understood where he'd gone wrong. It frightened him how much he was like his father. Screaming at his wife: the very thing he'd vowed never to do; the words he'd vowed never to say; the man he'd vowed never to become. Now he knows that if he wants to sink his roots deeper into Nicole's heart and mind, if he wants to keep her, it will be by learning when not to speak and what not to say.

Mike shakes his head and smiles down at the tabletop. This is the stuff about marriage that no one explains ahead of time, like the fine print on a loan. And while marrying Nicole has been a good thing, it's also been hard. Harder than he thought it would be. Harder, perhaps, than it has to be.

Nicole emerges from the corridor, scanning the dining room for her husband. She looks good, he thinks. The baby is just beginning to show. He knows she is self-conscious about it, worried what the pregnancy might do to her body. But he wants to see her body change. He thinks pregnant women are beautiful. He gives a little wave to catch her eye, and she sees him, though she does not return his smile.

—

The next afternoon, Randy wants to see Mike in his office. On the way down the hall, Mike stops for a cup of bad office coffee. He knows it'll be burnt and acidic after having sat around all morning, but he needs a little boost. When he enters Randy's small, windowless office, he is instructed to close the door. Randy sits behind a tiny desk, tapping a pen against the back of his hand. He's been looking over the latest sales reports. It's worse than expected. Mike's numbers are at rock bottom, and Randy wants an explanation.

"I'm in a slump, that's all. School and the baby—it's a lot."

"Yeah, the baby. How's the baby? How's your wife?"

"Well, we're . . ."

Randy lifts his eyebrows.

"It's all right," Mike says. "Everything is all right."

"Good. Glad that's not the problem. Because, well, there is a problem. A pretty serious problem." Randy jostles his necktie at the collar. "I just got out of a meeting where I got my ass chewed. My job is on the line. I'm not pretending."

"Okay." Mike takes a sip of acrid coffee; it's as bad as he thought.

"Something's got to change here, and I mean quick. We've got to start selling cars. So here's how it is: I want you here forty hours a week, every week. No more personal days, not unless it's an absolute fucking emergency. And I'm putting you back on nights, Tuesday to Saturday. Get you a little foot traffic, maybe you'll sell a car or two."

Mike's shoulders tighten. "I've got a night class next term."

"And I've got another quarter to lift sales around here, or I'm roadkill."

"The class is only offered once a year. I need it to graduate."

"Make the right choice, then," Randy says, turning his attention to the papers on his desk.

Mike walks back to his cubicle and throws himself into his chair with a sharp "Fuck!" Heads pop up from nearby desks. He hears some muttering. At that moment, he can't stand another second in that office. He phones the secretary at the front desk and tells her he's feeling ill. Then he storms out of the back door of the building, to the employee parking area. He drives around aimlessly for a while, trying to cool down, before stopping in at a bar for a drink. He's halfway through a whiskey sour when his cell phone rings. He reads the Caller ID line: it's Randy. He lets his voice mail pick it up, then retrieves the message a minute later. "Mike, where in hell did you go? Look, you better give me a call, or I'll have to write this up. You and me, we don't need that. Just give me a ring, okay?"

Mike deletes the message, then checks his watch. It's three o'clock. He turns off his phone and drops it in his coat pocket. He doesn't care if Randy writes him up. He doesn't care if he gets fired. Randy and the whole damn lot of them can go to hell. He finishes his drink and drives himself home.

Online, he finds a website offering testimonials of what it's like to raise a child with Trisomy 9. The hardships and the sacrifice. There are the worst cases, the severely disabled kids who need round-the-clock attention. Then there are the kids with developmental disabilities, lagging behind their peers. There are the medical bills, the second mortgages, the canceled vacations. Friends stop calling, stop coming around, because you're always caring for your child. He surfs through galleries of pictures, sees kids with oversized noses and sunken eyes, kids hooked up to breathing machines, kids wearing leg braces. There's a support group, a chat room, a number to call for more information. *You can do it*, one parent writes. *You can raise your child with this condition. You must give your all, but you can manage the situation.*

Is that the best you can hope for? Mike wonders. To manage the situation? He isn't sure he can commit to a life like that. What if your kid doesn't make it? You give over a year, maybe two, maybe a dozen—and the kid dies of liver failure, or his heart stops? Or he lives, but he's blind. Can't walk or talk. Can't breathe on his own. God knows what.

He knows they must decide. No matter what the tests show, good news or bad, they must decide. He and Nicole have always been pro-choice. He is still, at that moment, pro-choice. But he's seen the ultrasound images: the unmistakable curve of a human head; the tiny, ghostly hands. He's heard the drumming heartbeat. There's a human life inside of Nicole, no doubt about it. He's always written the pro-lifers off as a bunch of evangelical nut jobs. But maybe they're right. To terminate a pregnancy at twenty weeks, to undergo an abortion . . . He doesn't know if he can go so far as to call it murder.

But it might be.

Oh, Christ, he thinks. Would they have to visit one of those clinics like they show on TV? Could they go through that, being harassed by all those jerks with the bullhorns and the grisly photos? No, they'll go down to San Francisco. He'll pay whatever it costs to do it quietly, with some sort of dignity. That's if they can actually do it. Have an abortion. Somehow, it just doesn't seem possible.

He turns off the computer and throws himself onto the couch in the living room. Perhaps he's looking at this from the wrong end, he thinks. Perhaps this isn't a disaster but a great opportunity. Perhaps this is the moment toward which he, in his blind ignorance, has been led. For he considers himself a selfish, scattered man, trying to juggle too many plates at once. He worries too much about money, about advancing himself, about arranging the world on his own terms. It occurs to him, as it has on more than one occasion, that he'll never be happy. He'll always want more. He'll always wish things were somehow other than they actually are. He's never, not once in his life, been able to accept what he has and simply be content with it.

He recalls a time, years ago, when he flirted with Buddhism. He'd been dating a girl who regularly attended a Zen meditation group in town. Monks visited the group each month to give talks and offer spiritual counseling. Eventually, he requested a meeting. Not knowing any better, he treated it like a confessional. He admitted to cheating on his girlfriend. The monk's response was a lecture on karma: how, in this life, you are constantly working through the karmic consequences of this and other, inherited lives. It is your koan to struggle with this, the monk said. Your lust and selfishness. There is no escape from it. To acknowledge it, to admit it, these are the necessary first steps. But you must take the next step. You must work to clean up your karma, to leave this life having offered more good karma than bad.

"You could die never having cleared that stuff up," Mike said.

"That's true," the monk responded. "Many people do."

"What happens then?"

"The wheel of karma continues to turn," the monk explained. "Karma is passed to other beings. You, yourself, you might be reborn in a different realm. The animal world, perhaps. Or that of the hungry ghosts, beings who suffer insatiable hunger. Their bellies are immense, but their mouths are only as big as the eye of a needle."

Such talk struck Mike as bizarre. It depressed him, the thought that he might never free himself from the consequences of his actions. He quit visiting the group shortly thereafter. He and the girl didn't last much longer.

Now, it occurs to him that the monk might have been correct. He has been handed a kind of koan. He has finally bumped up against something from which he cannot simply turn tail and flee. Something he must face, if not embrace.

A boy, he mutters to himself. A son.

At dinner that evening, they sit across from each other at one end of the kitchen table, the other end of which is cluttered with Mike's school books and the day's mail. Nicole drags a finger across the nicked and scratched surface of the table. Mike knows she would like to replace it. And one day, when they can afford it, they will. But they need to make do for a little longer.

"How are you holding up?" he asks.

Nicole shakes her head. "This baby isn't normal. I haven't felt any kicking. Shouldn't it be moving around at twenty-one weeks? I think it might already be dead."

"No, I saw the ultrasound. He's in there, even if you can't feel him."

"Don't say 'him,'" she instructs.

"Right. Sorry." They have agreed not to announce the baby's sex to anyone. They will not use the pronouns "he" or "him," the preferred term being "Baby."

"Maybe we should just do it now," she says. "Do it and then move on."

"Before the tests come back? Then we won't know."

"We'll never know. That's what's driving me insane." She bangs a fist, lightly, against the tabletop. "Even if the tests come back okay, we'll never know. There will always be that slight chance."

"Life is full of slight chances. Sometimes you just have to take the risk."

"This isn't the ordinary kind of risk, you know that. This is extraordinary. This is beyond huge, and I can't stop thinking about it." She buries her face in her hands. "How can anyone live like this?"

He wipes his mouth with a napkin. "Think about what you're saying."

"I can't think." She lifts her face, fixing a sad, tired gaze on him. "You don't know what it's like, having this body. Growing a baby inside of you, knowing the baby might be sick. You don't 'think' anything. You feel it."

He reaches over and massages her shoulder, gently. "If the tests come back clean, we're probably okay. The odds are in our favor. Statistically."

"Statistically," she mutters. "Well, sweetheart, let me tell you. I don't feel okay, statistically."

"I'm just talking if the tests are clean," he says. "We can't terminate a baby at those odds."

She nudges a piece of broccoli to one side of her plate. "Maybe not. But if the tests show something?"

He stops massaging her shoulder, but leaves his hand there. "I think I want it, either way."

She folds her napkin, slowly, and places it neatly on the table. "I'm not raising a special-needs child. I'm not ready to throw my life off track for that."

"Maybe it's not throwing your life off track. Maybe it's finding a track. Reorienting your life, so you're not at the center." He sits forward, puts his elbows on the table. "I'm ready for it."

"Well, I'm not."

"Then you don't have to do it."

She meets his gaze. After a long moment, she shakes her head.

"You'd do it alone?"

"If I have to."

"You would divorce me."

"I didn't say that."

"But if I won't raise the child with you, it amounts to the same thing."

He touches his fingers to the stem of his wine glass. "That's up to you."

Her face screws up with pain and disbelief. "I'm going to forget you just said that." She leaves her meal half-eaten and walks down the hallway. Mike hears the bedroom door click shut. He's stunned by what they've just said, the territory that has suddenly opened before them. He's unsure how to proceed. He wonders if he should go to Nicole, comfort her. He could apologize, he knows that. But if she wants him to take his words back?

He looks up at the clock. It's seven. Too early, he thinks, to call it a night.

—

On Monday, Mike is summoned to the head manager's office for a little chat about teamwork and communication. He can only listen with one ear, distracted by the many photos littering his boss's desk. The kids in soccer uniforms, Boy Scout uniforms, or posed stiffly for a school portrait. The lecture finished, he duly apologizes, vowing to make a renewed effort, to consult Randy more frequently, to work that little bit extra. He and the head manager shake hands, and then he makes his way slowly through the maze of cubicles. Photos of bright, happy children grace every desktop, it seems. He pauses to study the artwork adorning the walls of a colleague, crude stick figures surrounded by oversized flowers and rainbows. Along the bottom of one picture, in block letters: I LOVE YOU SUPERDAD.

Everyone's got kids, he thinks. And everyone's kid is perfect. Why isn't his? This is supposed to be a happy time. His wife is pregnant with their first child and they are supposed to be hopeful. But they feel pushed into a deep, dark place.

Suddenly, terribly overcome with tears, Mike dashes to the men's room and locks himself in a stall. He weeps silently, into a wad of tissue. After a minute, he gathers himself. Blows his nose. He washes his face in the sink. If the tests don't come back clean, one of them will have to give in. That's the only way out of this mess. He's sure it will be him. How can he ask Nicole to take on something like this if her heart isn't fully in it? But to terminate a baby, even a baby with serious problems—it would destroy a piece of his soul. He isn't a religious man, he doesn't have strong convictions that way. Yet, in the past few days, a realization has slowly taken shape: if he has a responsibility in this world, if there is anything from which he cannot turn away, if there is anything he is ready to face, regardless of cost or consequence, this is it.

That afternoon, business at the car lot is slow. Mike knows he should spend that time catching up on paperwork, or studying specs for the new models, but he's thinking about how he and Nicole didn't speak all weekend, how Friday's quarrel hung between them like a booby trap. They didn't even *see* each other: he kept busy with schoolwork, writing an overdue term paper and catching up on reading, while Nicole ran off to brunch with one girlfriend, coffee with another, and the movies with a third. He feels horrible about it; he doesn't like playing these games. And though he doesn't know what to say, he's willing to make the first move. He phones Nicole at the law office, but she isn't picking up. He leaves a short message saying he loves her and he wants her to call. But she doesn't call. At six, he's off work and must dash to campus for a night class. He phones her cell as he drives across town but gets her voice mail. Ditto the home phone. He leaves messages, short and sweet.

In class, the professor reviews for next week's final exam. The first hour is fine, but then they plunge into neo-Keynesian economic theory, critiquing updated versions of the Phillips curve. Mike scribbles notes furiously. He knows he's missed a class or two. He knows he's fallen behind on the reading. But he didn't think it was *this* bad. If he fails the exam, he'll fail the class, which means he'll have to repeat it, which means delaying graduation yet again—unless he can cram a month's worth of study into a week. A week when his boss has all but threatened to fire him if he doesn't sell some cars. A week when he's waiting for the test results for his unborn son. A week when his wife won't speak to him.

It is half past ten when he pulls into the driveway of their home. Nicole's car is gone. She is rarely out this late on a work night. Another heart-to-heart with a girlfriend, he suspects. Well, at least she's talking to someone. She sure as hell isn't talking to him.

In the kitchen, he grabs a beer from the fridge. He tosses his keys on the table, and that is when he sees the note. As he reads, the back of his neck tightens like a sailor's knot. Nicole has driven up to Grass Valley to see her mother for a few days. She asks him not to call, to give her a little time and space to think. She needs a fresh perspective on things. *Please, don't give up on me*, she writes. *Don't give up on us. I'll call in a day or two, when I'm ready. I love you.*

Mike rereads the note several times, trying to understand what's happening. What is her mother saying to her right now, at that instant? The mother who gave her blessing to Nicole's first divorce. The mother who is herself once-divorced. The mother who, like any good parent, will back her daughter in whatever she decides to do.

He slams an open palm against the tabletop and bellows a curse into the emptiness of his home. He's been a damn fool!

Mike heads for the master bedroom, intent on changing out of his work clothes. As he enters the rear hallway, he stops before the first door on the right: the so-called store room—what will become, he hopes, the baby's room. At Nicole's request, they have kept the door shut at all times. They have deliberately delayed cleaning out the room, let alone set up a nursery. They have not purchased a crib or a bassinet or a changing table. No toys or little boy clothes. Nothing. Not a single thing. They've been living in a kind of fear, planning for the worst. Bracing themselves for something terrible.

He opens the door, flicks on the light, and steps into the room. It is cold. Last fall, he sealed the heating vent and stacked boxes on top of it, hoping to shave a few pennies off the heating bill. The boxes are labeled for their contents. Sweaters. Books. Holiday decorations. He kneels before a box with his name on it and pulls back the nested flaps. Inside are childhood toys: plastic model airplanes he built from kits, a G.I. Joe doll missing an arm. Farther down is a paper bag, its sides velvety with wear. He unfurls the lip of the bag. Inside is his collection of Matchbox toy cars, his single greatest obsession as a young child. The cars, dozens of them, are piled in a heap, all nicked and scratched, the wheels misaligned and the doors missing. He smiles. He and his pals beat the hell out of those cars, but it was a *world* they were creating. They built elaborate dirt tracks in the back yard, complete with tunnels, jumps, and improbably steep turns. They staged drag races, smash-up derbies, and Grands Prix. They invented names for their drivers, kept statistics, even had a little trophy for the day's winner. They got so worked up that fights would start. But they always forgave each other. They always came back to the game. Nobody ever quit for good.

Mike wakes early the next morning and showers. He brews a pot of coffee, toasts a bagel, and sits down with his economics textbook. He has a few hours to study before he has to be at work. But he can't focus. He spent most of the night tossing and turning, thinking about Nicole. Her note sits there on the table, atop yesterday's mail. He picks it up, re-reads it, then tosses it back down.

He stands and moves to the patio door. Outside, it is a gray, overcast morning. Rain blackens the concrete patio. He looks up into the trees, the branches bare and skeletal. A dozen crows are perched there. Their cawing, heard through the glass, is muted and soft. In the rain, the big, black birds appear strangely glossy. He watches them for several minutes, until one flies off. The others quickly follow. They might fly for miles, he thinks, until one alights on a fence or a rooftop. Then the others will gather around it. For crows are not solitary; they travel as a family, a flock. No, not a flock. What is the collective noun?

A murder of crows.

Mike grabs his car keys from the table, pats his jeans pocket to make sure he's carrying his wallet, then dons his winter coat. The trip to Grass Valley should take about two hours, though in winter you never know. If it's raining in the valley, it's snowing in the mountains. Either way, he's prepared for whatever Mother Nature throws at him. He has chains in the trunk and a full tank of gas. He hopes for clear roads and safe passage.

MY FAVORITE DISASTER

Chris Cook was the worst hockey player I'd ever seen. He could barely skate, his ankles bent like commas. He often pointed in the wrong direction on the ice. When he did go dig for a puck in the corner, some bruiser would flatten him against the boards and you'd need a spatula to peel him off. A hockey player expects to get hit. What's important is how quickly you return to play. Cook was always slow to get up, having lost a glove or his stick, which had been kicked behind the net. Worst of all was his puck-handling: the guy couldn't hit a Zamboni from twenty feet. Forget about clearing the zone. As a defenseman, he was about as effective as a sieve. We blew more third-period leads that year than I care to count.

In a Pee-Wee league every kid has to play, though no one says how much. If Cook saw more ice time than he should have, we all understood why: his stepfather was our coach. Bret Olsen was a local legend. He'd played for the Minnesota Golden Gophers back in the day, and rumor had it he nearly made the 1960 Olympic team. He played semi-pro in Canada for two seasons, and while he never climbed to the top level, he'd gone further than most. Every one of his players worshipped him.

Still, we grumbled whenever he put his stepson on the ice. Cook was second string, and though he played just a minute or two at a time, a lot can happen in a minute of hockey—and with Cook on the ice, it usually did. Naturally, he caught hell from the rest of the guys. And since many of us went to Washburn Elementary, we kept it up off the ice. The odd thing was, calling him names didn't work. Neither did pushing him around. You got no reaction. He'd just clam up and take it. There didn't seem to be any abuse he wouldn't tolerate. But every kid has his limit. You just have to push until you find it.

My mother and Sharon Olsen, Cook's mom, had grown up together, so when Sharon divorced her husband in Florida and returned to Duluth, my mother and Sharon happily picked up right where they'd left off. That made sense to me. What didn't make sense was why my mother assumed that Cook and I should be friends, too. Every time she asked me to call him up, I refused. Then, one afternoon as I sat in the kitchen eating a snack, my mother announced that we'd received an invitation to visit the Olsen house later that week.

I said forget it, I wouldn't go. When she asked why, I told her the truth: Cook was a dork, a serious weirdo. If anyone found out I'd been over to his house, I'd never live it down.

"But Sharon says he sits at your table in the classroom," my mother said. "He eats lunch with you every day. He's with you on the playground."

It was true. When he'd joined Mr. Johnson's fifth grade class, Cook had been assigned to Table Four with me and my best friend, Jerry Gustafson. I guess Cook thought that made him our pal. Every day, he followed us into the cafeteria and sat with us, uninvited. We ignored him. After lunch, he followed us onto the playground. We never asked him to join our games of boot hockey, ice football, or tag. He just hung back, trailing us, like a jackal. Watching.

After I'd told this to my mother, she gave me a long, hard look. "He's trying to fit in. Why won't you let him play?"

"Nobody's stopping him. He's never asked."

"That's his way of asking. You boys are cruel. Neither of you has ever invited him to do anything."

"Mom, he's a freak!"

A frown tightened in the corners of her mouth. "You don't know how disappointed I am to hear you say that, Jackie Rose. I want you to sit right there and think about this. When you've decided what kind of boy you're going to be, you come and let me know."

She left me there, in my chair in the kitchen, staring out the window into the back yard. I studied a patch of old snow, black and crusty with ice. I knew there was no way out of it, not after she'd put it like that. Still, I lingered, if only to deny my mother the satisfaction of seeing me fold too quickly.

We called Jerry Gustafson, our right winger, "The Little Tornado." Jerry wasn't the best player on the ice; we had faster skaters, we had guys with better stick-handling skills. I understood the strategy of the game better than most, including Jerry. What he had was something that can make a good hockey player occasionally great: blood hunger.

A cross-check from Jerry was like hitting a brick wall. A scrappy player, he jabbed at opponents with the tip of his stick. He spent a lot of time in the penalty box, but when he was on the ice he made things happen. His slapshots from the blue line were incendiary. He'd rear back with his stick and the next thing you knew the puck was dropping from the high corner of the net, the goalie shaking his head in disbelief. He hadn't even seen the damn thing.

But that wasn't why we called Jerry the Little Tornado. That came when somebody made the mistake of hitting him wrong, or trash-talking him too much. In a second, his stick was on the ice, the gloves were off, and he was lighting into the kid. Jerry threw punches like a machine gun. Black eyes, broken teeth, scratches and cuts: he wore them like badges.

Though Jerry was my best friend and lived just four blocks away, I didn't like to go to his house. His dad drove a city bus on second shift. His mother worked across the bridge, deep in Wisconsin, and was home late every night. After school, Jerry stayed with his older brother Dean, who constantly tormented him. Or me, when I stopped by. Once, Dean convinced me to sniff a handful of black pepper. I spent the next hour sneezing my head off. The asshole got a real kick out of that.

Jerry and Dean hated each other. They fought constantly. I once saw Dean throw a ski pole at Jerry like a javelin, narrowly missing his head. Another time, I watched him grab Jerry's arm and wrench it behind his back, lifting him straight off the ground. Jerry screeched with pain, tears pouring out of his eyes. I thought his arm would pop off. Not that Dean would care.

Next day, Jerry hit his brother in the back of the head with a piece of firewood, just cold-cocked him without warning. Dean spent two days in the hospital with a concussion. And though Jerry caught hell for that, we all knew he'd do it again. Whatever coldness it is that allows people to treat each other that way, Jerry Gustafson had it in him.

My mother and I visited the Olsen house on a Thursday afternoon. While the women sipped coffee in the kitchen, I followed Cook to his room. The walls were plastered in *Star Wars* movie posters, pages torn from fan magazines, even toy packaging. If it had anything to do with that film, it had been taped up. His dresser-tops and bookshelves were cluttered with plastic dolls of Han Solo, Luke Skywalker, C-3PO, and all the rest. Spacecrafts and troop carriers covered the floor. In the largest poster on his wall, Darth Vader stood, feet apart, his red light saber glowing. Behind him loomed the Death Star.

Cook asked me how many times I'd seen the movie.

"Just once," I said.

"I saw it fourteen times." He stared at me. Cook was tall and stick-thin, with a mop of snot-colored hair and a bony, haunted look about his face.

I pointed at the poster. "It was cool when the Death Star blew up that planet."

"Alderaan. Home of Princess Leia and seat of the Rebel Alliance."

"Right, yeah." The last movie I'd watched was *The Bad News Bears Go to Japan*. I asked Cook if he'd seen it. He hadn't. "Not as good as the first two," I said, "but still pretty funny."

Cook pointed to the plastic action figures on his bookshelf. "Do you want to stage some combat? You could lead a rag-tag rebel squad on a suicide mission to destroy the Death Star. I'll command the superior forces of the Empire."

I looked around the room, trying to find anything that wasn't related to *Star Wars*. I asked if he liked baseball. It was going to be a tough year for the Twins, I said. We'd just traded Rod Carew to the California Angels. "Who've we got left? Roy Smalley at shortstop. At least he's got a bat. And Dave Goltz pitching. But that's about it."

Cook raised a finger to his lips, as if considering this. "A Wookie's diet is rather interesting," he said, and went off on that.

"How about we go outside," I interrupted. "Maybe toss a ball around."

He said he didn't usually play outside. Too many bugs.

"Bugs? In February?"

He shrugged his shoulders. "Want to see my pod racer?"

On the bookshelf stood a Darth Vader doll, arm upraised, before a squad of white-helmeted Storm Troopers. I reached over and flicked Darth on the head, toppling him. A half-dozen soldiers fell, too, like so many dominoes. Cook frowned. I raised my eyebrows and bounced on my heels. Cook reached in and carefully re-positioned the dolls. "The Death Star had 768 tractor beam generators," he told me, then listed the numbers of assault shuttles and blast-boats stationed there, as if I cared.

Finally, I said I had to go to the bathroom and walked down the hall. When my mother found me thirty minutes later, I was flipping through an issue of *Sports Illustrated* in Coach Olsen's study. Later, at home, she asked why we boys hadn't played together.

"All he talks about is *Star Wars*."

"So? All you talk about is hockey and baseball."

I knew it wasn't the same. I just didn't know how to explain it. My mother lectured me on being a guest in another person's home, then sent me to my room to "think it over."

I promptly stuck my nose in a book. That winter, I was obsessed with natural disasters. Earthquakes, tsunamis, hurricanes: I studied them all. But my favorite was a volcano. For sheer destructive force, nothing could match it. When Mount Pelée exploded in 1902, an entire town in Martinique disappeared within a minute, buried under lava and ash; just two men survived. In 1783, the Laki eruption killed twenty-five percent of Iceland's population. Such accounts frightened and excited me in odd ways, prompting apocalyptic daydreams of elaborate proportions. I imagined myself standing alone on the shore of Lake Superior, ash raining from a colorless sky. On the hill above me, my vacant, wasted city. At my feet, a defiant spring flower. Like me, a lone survivor.

Surprisingly, our hockey team advanced in the city tournament to the quarter finals. No Glen Avon squad had made it that far in ten years, and none had ever won the whole shebang. There was a palpable buzz around the locker room. Kids at school patted us on the back and wished us the best of luck. Jerry and I talked about it endlessly, speculating about what would happen if we actually won the tournament. Our team would be on the front page of *The Duluth Tribune.* We'd have trophies the size of the Enger Tower.

Maybe we'd meet the mayor, Jerry said.

"Forget the mayor," I blurted. "I want to meet Curt Giles." Giles, a star player on the UMD Bulldogs, was scheduled to talk at the awards ceremony. Giles was a defenseman, one of my tribe. I'd watched him from the upper tiers of the Duluth Arena-Auditorium, studying his moves like a scientist. He was short and slight like me, but he skated hard and cross-checked harder. Nobody fought better in the corner for a puck. Nobody cleared the zone faster. Giles was the real deal; he was who I wanted to be on the ice.

In the quarterfinals we faced Congdon East, a team we'd often played. We were evenly matched going in. In the first period, each team scored a goal. Then we exploded in the second: Jerry scored one, and then our center flicked a beautiful little wrist shot into a gap about the size of your thumb. The place went nuts. We entered the third period ahead, 3-1. Coach Olsen ordered the first string on the ice for the start of the period. He was trying to be cool and collected, but he was as excited as anyone. In the team box, no one was sitting down. Even Cook stood at the boards, urging us on.

The puck had been shot into my corner. I handily evaded a hip check from a slow left winger and skated the puck to center ice, where I passed it to Jerry, who crossed the blue line and let loose with a slapshot that missed high, sailing over the boards. A whistle blew, ending the play. A split-second later, a Congdon winger blindsided Jerry, sending him sprawling to the ice. His stick flew halfway to the boards. In an instant, the Little Tornado was on his feet, charging for the kid. Helmets and gloves flew off as from a centrifuge. The referee blew his whistle a dozen times. He was a big guy, and he had no trouble breaking up the fight. But Jerry couldn't cool it. He kept trying to break free and take another swing. The ref stiff-armed him, pushing him farther back. That's when Jerry took a swing at the ref, a sloppy roundhouse that barely grazed the guy's left ear, but still. You never swing at the ref.

Immediately, both coaches were on the ice. Olsen pinned Jerry to the boards, screaming in his face that he was out of line. Jerry was ejected from the game, of course. Coach put the second string in, and sure enough

Congdon East bulldozed Cook and scored a goal. Coach Olsen was furious; it was the only time I heard him yell at his stepson, ordering him off the ice.

"Rose," he barked at me, "get out there and play left defense. You're in for the rest of the game." I was winded, and a little shaken up by the fact that Jerry had been ejected, but I went out there and gave my all, putting up a stonewall defense that no forward could penetrate. When the final whistle blew, we'd won, 3-2. We would play in the semi-finals next weekend—and at the Arena-Auditorium, no less. We were beside ourselves with joyous disbelief.

Except for Jerry. Coach Olsen benched him for the next game. He announced it in the warming house, in front of everyone. Jerry sat in the corner, hanging his head, ignoring everything around him. I felt for him, sure. But I was mad at him, too. Without him on the ice next week, our chances against Hermantown were that much lower. But Coach Olsen was right, and I admired him for having the guts to stand on principle, no matter what it meant to his team.

That winter, all students in Mr. Johnson's class had to deliver an oral report on a current event. We suffered mangled accounts of Patty Hearst's release from prison, the meltdown at Three Mile Island, and the rise of Margaret Thatcher. Half the time, it was hard to hear the presentation over the sound of Johnson's snoring in the back of the room.

Not so Chris Cook. He stood before us in a copper-colored hardhat and a khaki fishing vest, his pockets stuffed with a compass, waterproof matches, and a monstrous Swiss Army knife (you know, the one with the eating utensils and scissors). He toted an orange plastic tool box filled with water purification tablets, salt pills, and genuine K-rations. But the whopper was his Geiger counter—a *real* Geiger counter. God knows where he got it. I guess you can buy those things, but why any eleven-year-old would even think about it is beyond me.

Cook had pasted an enormous world map to a board. Across the top, in fat black letters, he'd written SKYLAB IS FALLING. We'd all heard about Skylab, of course. In 1979, it was big news: the aging, abandoned space station was gradually slipping out of its low-earth orbit and, at some point later in the year, would enter the atmosphere and disintegrate. Almost certainly, some debris would make it through. Red-hot, molten metal—chunks as big as a car—could fall virtually anywhere, Cook explained. If Skylab entered the atmosphere over western Russia, for instance, the wreckage would scatter like pepper from the Yukon to the Great Lakes.

"According to my calculations, this would mean a trail of carnage coming out of Ontario, through Duluth, and reaching as far as Washington, D.C.," Cook stated. "I've written to President Carter, warning him to stay out of the White House until August first."

"Where's he supposed to go?" somebody asked.

"I suggest NORAD headquarters." Cook described a military city hidden under the Rocky Mountains, near Denver, with enough food and water for a year. "The president has an apartment there, completely furnished. He can monitor the world via satellite communi—"

"—Thank you, Mr. Cook," interrupted Mr. Johnson. "That's very enlightening. What is your final conclusion?"

"Be prepared," Cook said, rapping his knuckles against his hard hat. He held up his survival kit and Geiger Counter. Naturally, the class erupted in laughter. Cook stood before us, eyes darting about. Though I mocked him with the rest of my peers, I was secretly awed by his presentation—the sheer terror of the threat. I couldn't get it off my mind.

Unfortunately, talking to Cook was impossible. For weeks after his presentation, he wore that absurd costume to school. Always a loner, he'd made himself a pariah, a genuine freak case. He no longer shadowed us at lunch or during recess. Jerry had driven him off. Cook kept to himself, walking along the back fence of the playground, measuring for radiation with his Geiger counter. One day, Jerry and I sat on a bench along one end of the field, watching him. I cautiously suggested that his Skylab presentation had been the best so far.

"It's a bunch of crap," Jerry said.

"I don't know. What if he's right?" I told him that a giant meteorite had slammed into a remote portion of Siberia in 1908, flattening trees in every direction for 800 miles. "If that thing had hit four hours later, it would've wiped out St. Petersburg."

Jerry gave me a look like I'd just told him two plus two equaled five.

"I read it in a book," I said, quietly.

"Cook is an asswipe," Jerry growled. "And so are you, if you think he's right."

I sat forward, shoulders hunched, and studied a line of ants marching blindly in the dirt. "Ah, forget about Cook." I pointed to a boot hockey game across the playground. "Let's go show 'em how it's done."

"Yeah, let's go fuck it up," Jerry said, standing. Together we ran over there, placing ourselves on opposite sides, eager to dominate the game as always.

On Friday mornings we studied American history. Mr. Johnson asked us to open our history books to Chapter Twelve, the Constitutional Convention. For me, the next hour was wonderful. Fifth grade was the year that school had become fun. I no longer cringed when we were assigned a book report or an experiment. I paid close attention to class lectures. That day, Mr. Johnson discussed the relative merits of the Virginia Plan, the New Jersey Plan, and Hamilton's plan, which was really just a rehashed British Parliament. All of this led to the Connecticut Compromise, which gave us the House of Representatives and the Senate as we know them today. Mr. Johnson dimmed the lights and showed us color slides of paintings depicting various orators, the signing of the Constitution, and so on. It was great stuff, and I was eating it up. Meanwhile, Jerry goosed me under the desk, trying to draw me in with fart noises and such. Ordinarily, this would have been amusing. But I'd come to resent it. It had occurred to me that my best friend didn't care about school at all; not one single subject interested him. He never read books, had to be badgered to turn in his homework, and took a perverse pride in failing tests. I didn't see the point. Worse, I knew Jerry didn't have one.

The lights came on and paper was distributed. We were to draw a picture depicting some aspect of the Constitutional Convention: a building, a document, the Founding Fathers. In our textbook was a photograph of Independence Hall, which I copied as best I could. Across from me sat Chris Cook, head bowed over his paper. He seemed so focused and intense. I asked to see his picture. He held up a portrait of Benjamin Franklin which he'd copied out of the book, freehand. He had everything perfect: the tri-cornered hat sitting on his head like a piece of pie, the bulbous nose, the slight smile in the corner of the mouth that made him look like a wise-ass. I was impressed, and I said so. Cook sat back in his chair, smiling sheepishly.

"Hey, Jer, look at that." I pointed at Cook's picture.

"Looks like a dork," Jerry said. "A dork with UFO for a hat."

The smile dropped off Cook's face.

"Jerry wouldn't know a good drawing if it hit him in the ass," I said. "That's really good."

"Thanks," Cook muttered, softly. He lowered his head back to his work.

"Now check *this* out," Jerry said, pushing his picture across the table. He had drawn George Washington laying an enormous turd in the middle of Independence Hall, under which he'd scribbled the chapter title from our textbook: "The Fruit of Democracy." I couldn't help but laugh.

Mr. Johnson asked the table leaders to collect the drawings. Jerry was our leader that week, so he took our art and turned it in. Later, when the bell rang for recess, Johnson made our table stay behind. He waited until the room emptied, then stood before us, arms folded across his big chest. He asked Cook if he was responsible for "The Fruit of Democracy."

"W-what?" Cook stammered. "I drew Ben Franklin."

"Liar," Jerry snarled.

I gave Jerry a questioning look, but he ignored it.

"Mr. Cook, your name is on the work in question," Johnson said, holding it up for us to see. CHRIS COOK had been penciled crudely in the corner. That it was a forgery seemed plain enough. But Johnson was after something. "Did you or did you not draw this picture?"

Cook sat like a deer in the headlights. He knew that if he ratted out Jerry he'd get his ass whipped. He actually started to shake and sniffle, the wuss.

"I . . . I don't remember."

"Search your memory, boy. It was just minutes ago. You can't possibly have forgotten."

"Sir, I . . ."

"It was him," Jerry said, pointing at Cook.

"That's enough, Mr. Gustafson." Johnson pursed his dry, colorless lips. "Mr. Rose, have you anything to say?"

Under the desk, Jerry kicked my shin, hard. Like Cook, I knew what disloyalty would garner, not that I was afraid to hit back. No, I sat there listening to Cook snivel like the cornered mouse that he was, and it made me resent him. Why couldn't he stand up for himself? It almost seemed like his fault that this was happening. If he weren't such a damn pussy, it'd all be over in a second.

I looked at Jerry, his eyes fierce and commanding. I straightened in my chair. "Chris drew it," I said.

Cook looked at me like I'd just strangled his cat. Then he burst into tears, shoulders heaving. Johnson dismissed me and Jerry, but held Cook for further questioning. Jerry and I burst out of the classroom, tear-assing down the hallway, hollering like cavemen, the taste of the kill fresh on our lips.

Our celebration was premature. By day's end, Jerry and I had been called individually to the principal's office. Under more intense scrutiny, I confessed. I was slapped with a lunch detention for lying, but Jerry was given a one-day, at-home suspension. That seemed harsh, but then Jerry did have a long rap sheet with the principal, mostly for fighting. He would miss school on Monday. On the walk home that afternoon, he started calling it his "little vacation," as if he'd accomplished something.

The next morning, Saturday, I rose early and suited up for our game against Hermantown. During the drive downtown, my mother reamed me about my detention. Not only had I lied, I had embarrassed her. I'd finked on her best friend's kid, and now she had to spend an entire morning with both parents, and what was she supposed to say to them? I didn't know what to tell her. I was trying to focus on the playoffs.

The game was a disaster. From the first drop of the puck, everything felt wrong. Playing in the Arena-Auditorium, where I'd seen so many UMD games, was anything but inspiring. Staring up from the rink into that canyon of empty seats made it feel like we were playing in a crypt. Jerry sat with us in the team box, suited up and ready to go, but Coach Olsen stuck to his promise. The Little Tornado never left the bench. That brought us all down; our hearts just weren't in it. Two men short (Bobby Sanders had the stomach flu), our first string couldn't carry the weight, and the second stringers struggled to fill the gaps. Coach moved me up to left wing, which meant Cook was on the ice for most of the game. It's a wonder we held them to 4-1.

In the locker room afterwards, Coach Olsen gave a short speech. We hadn't played our best, he said. He didn't mind the loss so much as the fact that we hadn't shown up to win. That was inexcusable. "Always give your all, boys," he told us. "At least then, win or lose, you'll be proud of yourselves." Then he lectured us on what it meant to be a team. "Some of you, and you know who you are, have been less than fraternal with one another. For me, that's more disappointing than anything. In order to win, a team has to work together, help each other out—on and off the rink. If you don't have that . . . " He paused, considering his words. Then he shook his head, said he'd see us at the awards banquet in two weeks, and left us to pack up our gear.

The locker room was quiet as a church. If I didn't actually crawl out of there on my belly, I should have. I felt like a bug.

On Tuesday, the day after his suspension, Jerry sat quietly at our table in the corner of the room, hands tucked under his armpits, scowling like an old drunk. After about an hour of this, I asked him what was up. All he said was that his brother Dean had stayed home with him yesterday. He didn't have to tell me any more. I knew well enough what Monday had been like.

We had math that morning. During the worksheet exercises, Jerry's pencil lead snapped. I watched as he walked across the room to Table Seven, where Chris Cook had been re-assigned. Jerry plucked the pencil out of Cook's hand, then tossed his broken one at him. Naturally, Cook missed the catch. Without a word, he reached down, collected the pencil, and walked off to sharpen it.

Jerry returned to his seat, a big grin on his face.

"What's your problem?" I said. "You better watch it. Johnson's got your number."

"Johnson can suck my dick."

When Cook finished at the sharpener, he didn't return to his seat. He walked to our table and placed Jerry's newly-sharpened pencil on the desktop. Eyes fixed on the floor, he said, "That wasn't cool. Don't do it again, or I'll tell." Then he held a hand out, waiting for his pencil.

I sat straight up, eyes wide. Without looking at Cook, Jerry said, very quietly, "Get out of here before I shove this thing up your ass."

At the front of the class, Mr. Johnson stood from behind his desk. "Boys, what's going on? Mr. Cook, you will return to your seat. You are not to talk to Mr. Gustafson or Mr. Rose at this time."

Though he trembled, Cook stayed put, hand extended.

"If I come over there," Johnson boomed, "all three of you will regret it."

Jerry handed over his pencil and Cook quietly returned to his table. Did the earth open up and swallow me whole? It must have. Jerry rarely backed down from anyone, let alone the likes of Chris Cook.

When the lunch bell rang, I followed Jerry on our usual rounds. His mood was not hard to discern. He slammed open doors, kicked at gravel on the sidewalk, and spat a huge loogie on the flag pole. In the past, I would've tried to cheer him up, or at least get him talking. But I decided to ignore him. When he was like that, he was no fun, and anyway he'd been a royal jerk. Instead of tagging behind the sour prince, I did something I never did: I left him sitting alone at our picnic table in the far corner of the field and joined a game of touch football that was just starting up.

Ten minutes later, Jerry walked right through the middle of our game, eyes fixed dead ahead, ignoring our shouts and complaints. We watched him cross the field. Chris Cook was back there, wandering among the birch trees, talking to himself, waving his Geiger counter around. Jerry stood before him, legs spread, and yelled something. Startled, Cook turned, though he couldn't look Jerry in the eye. Naturally, we all followed, forming a circle a few feet back. Jerry was going on about Chris having ratted him out, about being a little suck-face narc. Cook shook his head, his gaze a few feet off to one side.

"Look at me when I'm talking to you," Jerry said. And when Cook didn't, Jerry took a step forward and shoved him. Cook quivered like a string puppet. "Look at me, douche bag." Jerry went up on his toes, put both hands against Cook's chest, and gave him a shove that sent him sprawling. His copper helmet spun off like a wounded top.

A few kids laughed. Cook lay there, completely helpless. Jerry took a step forward, challenging his victim to get up and fight. His face was crimson, his fists already clenched. I knew better than anyone what he was about to do and how bad it was going to be. So I did the only thing I could imagine doing. I tackled Jerry to the ground and slugged him in the kidneys—a real, honest-to-God punch. He responded with a knee to my gut, and then his hot, grubby hand was in my face, and that was it. We rolled around in the dirt, getting in kicks and punches wherever we could, scratching at necks, pulling hair. The circle of kids formed around us, cheering us on. We went at it, blind in our fury. Two friends fighting, that's the worst. Because once it's started, it can't end nicely. Jerry was my better in both weight and strength. I got a few good licks in early, but soon he was on top of my chest, pressing his kneecaps painfully into my biceps. He took my head in his meaty hands and smashed the back of my skull against the ground like it was a coconut. Then he leaned forward, put his forearm across my windpipe and pressed down. I couldn't breathe. My lungs felt like two hot burning bags, ready to explode. I kicked desperately with my feet, twisted my hands around, tried to shake him off with my hips. But Jerry was too heavy. His face loomed over mine, his eyes wide and manic, teeth bared. I gasped in a futile effort to draw a clear breath. I thought my eyes would pop out of my head.

Finally, the yard duty peeled Jerry off me. It took two of them to haul him, snarling like a feral cat, into the office. I lay on the ground, unable to stand, sucking desperately for air. Something felt very wrong in my windpipe. My breath came slow and tight, with a slight wheeze. My head was already ringing; my heart pounded like a kettle drum. I had scratches up and down my arms and neck, drops of blood already beading. Someone helped me to my feet. I walked, a little unsteady, on my own to the office. Outside the ring of kids watching the aftermath, Chris Cook wandered off along the fenceline, helmet back on his head, Geiger counter in hand, lost again in his world of daydream, some place where he felt safe from heartache, consequence, and the dagger-sharp eyes of others. I knew he'd never thank me, not that I deserved it. I hadn't saved him.

TELL ME WHERE YOU ARE

Peterson paced in the front hallway as his wife primped and preened before the mirror. She wore a silk blouse tightly tucked into a short black skirt, and a push-up bra. Black stockings highlighted her shapely calves. It was Thursday. She had her night class at the university. She usually wore jeans and a simple blouse. But tonight was special, she said, a big occasion.

Peterson folded his arms across his chest. "Who is this guy, anyway? You don't have to get dolled up for him."

"I told you, his name is Michael Munro. He's a classmate." Lifting her chin, she carefully applied her lipstick. "We're giving a presentation tonight. You have to look the part. You don't get a second chance at first impressions."

"You mean with your professor."

She recapped her lipstick and dropped it in her bag. "Of course."

"Then you're going out for a drink."

Lori sighed. "With the girls, as usual."

"You'll have your cell? When you go out?"

She nodded. "Call only in an emergency."

"I want to know how your thing goes."

"It'll go fine, you know that." She turned to him, one hand planted on a curvy hip. "Tell me how I look."

Peterson gave her a quick once-over: a tall woman with great legs and a high, tight bust. He tried to remember the last time she'd dressed like that for him. They hadn't had a night out, just the two of them, in months. There was always an excuse. Night school. Homework. For the last month, she and her classmate had been meeting on Saturday afternoons, working on their project. She often stayed late, missing dinner at home.

He said, "You look like a million bucks."

"Do I look like I want to *make* a million bucks? Not that an English professor knows about making money." She smiled facetiously. "Kidding! You know that. Give me a kiss. Here," she said, pointing to a spot beside her mouth. He leaned in and pecked her on the cheek. Her perfume smelled brassy and sharp—a new scent, not one he recognized.

She put a hand on the front door and turned to him one last time. "Wish me luck."

"Break a leg," Peterson muttered. And then she was gone. He stood at the front window of their house and watched her drive down the avenue in her aging Honda Accord. He followed her red tail lights to the intersection, where she joined in traffic without indicating her turn.

At the kitchen bar, Peterson poured himself a bourbon over ice. In the family room, seven-year-old Rachel sat on the couch, hair in pigtails, staring at the television. Barney the purple dinosaur danced oafishly in a circle, fat arms flopping at his sides, singing "I love you, you love me, we're a happy family." Behind him trailed a line of handsome children: one black, one Latino, one Asian. A white kid in leg braces hobbled behind them like a drunken robot. Rachel sang along in a high, bird-like warble. When Barney waved good-bye, she waved back.

There is no cruelty quite like the illusion of a perfect world, Peterson thought.

He walked down the hall to his small office. On the desk were piles of student papers waiting to be graded. There was tomorrow's lesson to prepare. And, up on a shelf above the desk, a small pile of papers waiting to be assembled into job applications—his way of planning for the worst. He was up for tenure at his university, and it didn't look good. On last year's review, he'd been warned about his lack of publications. Teaching, teaching—that bottomless belly of the beast—was his only savior. But the last person to get tenure based solely on teaching had been hired during the Reagan administration.

His prospects for a new job were dim. To have a real shot, he'd have to be willing to start over, to reset the tenure clock, and to accept a higher teaching load. We'd better be practical, he'd told Lori. We should talk about what's next, where we might go. He made jokes about Mississippi, North Dakota, or, god forbid, Texas.

But Lori wasn't having it. She reminded him that she'd spent seven years working dead-end jobs in Minneapolis to put her husband through graduate school. Moving to California had been a kind of sweet reward, and she wasn't about to give it up. They had a home there. Rachel was in the first grade. They had friends, or at least Lori had friends. She was in the second year of her MBA program. The bank where she worked was paying half of her tuition. And she liked her job. There'd been talk of a promotion, a possible move into middle-management. Peterson might have blown his big opportunity, she told him, but he wasn't going to spoil hers. "You want to move to Mississippi?" she said. "Go ahead. You'd have to kill me first."

Maybe, thought Peterson.

Maybe he'd get tenure without promotion. That happened sometimes. Just before turning in his review file, he'd sent out a flurry of last-minute submissions to some scholarly journals, old stuff culled from his dissertation. It was crap, really, with no chance of seeing print. Maybe the committee would cut him a break. If not, there was always Plan B: join the English Department's pool of part-timers, queuing up behind former students, faculty spouses, and other clingers-on. Forever scrambling for a full-time schedule. Forever teaching Freshman Composition. Forever the guy who used-to-be.

An ice cube in his bourbon popped and cracked, then sank to the bottom of his glass.

From up above the ceiling, in the attic, came a distressingly familiar sound: a thin, sharp scraping, like a fingernail against a block of wood. He cocked his ear, trying to place it. It seemed to be in a far corner of the room, over by the window. The sound of mice gnawing on wood, chewing his house to bits from the inside out.

He set his empty glass on a bookshelf. He walked quickly to the garage, from which he took a folding ladder. In the back hallway of the house, flashlight in hand, he ascended the ladder, its supports wobbling unevenly on the tiled floor below, and lifted himself into the attic. It smelled vaguely sour, ammoniacal. He shined the light around him. Rodent droppings were scattered all over the insulation and the exposed joists and beams. Quite a lot more than he remembered. Surely not the work of just a few mice, as he'd originally thought. This was an infestation. The little bastards were chewing holes in his siding, or his roof tiles, or right through the damn ceiling. God only knew what they were eating up there, or how many litters they'd birthed in his batting and insulation. Well, it was his own damn fault. He'd been slow to respond, listening to the gnawing and scratching for weeks before running to the hardware store for a "Mouse Control Kit." A week ago, he'd set out a series of traps. And then promptly forgot about the matter.

He shined his light onto the little platform where he'd set out four glue traps, baited with crackers. The traps were gone. How far could a stuck mouse drag a tray full of glue? And where would it go? He swept his flashlight beam across the attic. The darkness beyond the dim bulb's reach was Conradian. He sensed an army of rodents out there, huddling in the eaves, munching on his crackers, sniggering.

He crawled on all fours along a joist, making his way to the furnace duct, alongside which he'd placed two traps, little black plastic jobs that snapped together like an angry lizard's jaw, breaking the rodent's neck. The remaining trap was shut and empty. It had been chewed nearly to bits, the thick plastic covered in deep, methodical gouges. Peterson looked closely at the size of the teeth marks, then looked again at the droppings scattered around him. Of course! The problem was not mice, but rats: a different caliber of foe, requiring different tactics.

He lowered himself gingerly down the step ladder and replaced the access panel. He washed his hands in the bathroom, two minutes of vigorous scrubbing in hot water, the soap lathered on like shaving cream. He wasn't sure which angered him more: the fact that he had rats in his attic, or the fact that he'd misjudged his opponent. And now, due to his indolence and procrastination, the problem was nearly out of hand.

He looked himself over in the mirror, studied the dark circles beneath his eyes, the two-day stubble covering his cheeks and neck. He must take charge of the situation. Immediately.

Peterson poured another bourbon. In the family room, Rachel was into the next show, something with kids heating glass beakers over Bunsen burners. White smoke puffed up like dragon's breath. What in hell was PBS airing these days? Little Bombmakers, or Meth Family Robinson? He asked Rachel how she was doing, and if she was hungry.

She nodded, then said her mother had just called.

"She did? Why didn't you get me?"

"I couldn't find you. She was on her break from class. She said her thingie went good."

"Went well," Peterson corrected her. But Rachel, sweet nymph, had already turned back to her show.

Peterson checked his watch. It was seven-thirty. Lori might still be on break. He went into the kitchen and picked up the phone and dialed his wife's cell number. He got her voice mail. "Hi, you've reached Lori Myers-Peterson. Please leave a message." Since returning to school, she'd changed her greeting. She now used her maiden name, hyphenating it with her married name. Something about her academic records being in that name and not wanting to pay the fees required to change it. She was Lori Myers, academically speaking. That was how her professors and fellow students knew her.

After the beep, Peterson spoke. "Lori, honey, glad your presentation went well. Our problem is worse than I'd thought. We've got rats, not mice. Rats in the attic. I need to talk to you. Call before you go out. Thanks." A second later, he added, "It's urgent," then disconnected.

In the family room, Peterson abruptly turned off the television set. This brought forth a shrill complaint from his daughter, who sprang from the couch like a startled cat.

"Grab your coat, baby," he said, "there's a slice of hot pizza in it for you, if you help Daddy on his mission."

He watched, heartened, as his daughter bravely choked back her tears. She loved pizza and hadn't had it in weeks. "What mission?"

"Rodents," he said, "or control thereof. Now grab your coat and let's roll!"

At the hardware store, Todd the Friendly Service Representative explained that if it was rats in your attic, and if complete extermination was your goal, there was really only one option: poison bait pellets. "Just don't let the little one near the stuff," he said, pointing to Rachel. "It's lethal. But oh so simple to use. Set out two or three bait trays, and the rats will come to you, sir. They love it! Guaranteed! Or we will gladly offer you store credit."

"How's it work, exactly?" Peterson asked.

The poison induces severe hemorrhaging, Todd explained. The rat literally burns its guts out, bleeding to death in four to five days.

"Does that hurt the rat?" Rachel asked.

"It sure doesn't feel good!" said Todd, with a wink. He handed Peterson the green box.

Rachel wrapped an arm around Peterson's waist and gave her father a mournful look, which he chose to ignore. At the checkout, he picked up a Leatherman, a seventy-five-dollar tool that folded and unfolded in curious ways, with more features than a Swiss Army knife. It was the sort of tool that told people you were handy, that you knew how to do things, that you took good care of your home. That you were capable that way.

Rachel's favorite pizza parlor was a big, boxy place with a cheerful rodent for its mascot. Peterson laughed. Go ahead and smile, you smug bastard! Tonight you die!

The parlor had an indoor playground. The plastic play structure was grubby with countless children's fingerprints and smelled faintly of sweat and BO. Lori would never let Rachel play there. But Peterson was different. Looser, he liked to think. Kids were supposed to get dirty. And this kid could use a little exercise! Peterson loitered on a bench while Rachel zoomed down the slide or dangled from the monkey bars. She laughed and skipped around, singing the Barney theme song. Peterson smiled and encouraged her. He was thankful for this part of his life, a wonderful daughter with two parents who loved her deeply. And as long as he phrased it that way, as long as the narrative stopped right there, it seemed like a good life.

As they waited for their pizza, Peterson played a few arcade games with his daughter. They played air hockey and tossed miniature basketballs. Peterson wasn't much interested in the games until they got to the Bop-A-Gopher. Peterson conked the furry animals on their skulls with the red hammer, one after the other, with a relish and dexterity that surprised even him. He took a savage glee in it, bells ringing and lights flashing ever faster as he pounded, cracked, and thwacked the heads. He scored enough points to win a stuffed animal, the pizzeria's rodent mascot dressed up like a gold miner. Rachel looked at the thing contemplatively, then said it was mean to poison a rat.

"Yes, I suppose it is," Peterson said. "But rats are dirty and sometimes carry disease. They poop in your attic and chew on your electrical wires and damage the siding of your house. A problem like that—you have to stop it right away, as quickly as you can."

"But do you have to *kill* them?"

"Yes." A moment later, he added, "I'm sorry, honey." He poured another beer from his pitcher. The foam rose quickly to the lip of his glass, but stopped there. "It's part of being a grown-up. Sometimes we do mean things. But you have to ask why you're doing that thing. If the reason is a good one, like keeping our house clean and safe, then the mean act is justified."

"What's 'justified'?"

"Acceptable. When you have a good reason to do a bad thing, you say it's justified."

"But it's still a bad thing." She pushed a game token around the tabletop in a circle. "Are you and Mommy getting a divorce?"

Peterson stiffened. "Why do you ask that?"

"I heard Mommy on the phone. Talking about divorce."

"Who was she talking to?"

"I don't know."

"She was probably talking about somebody else."

"You guys argue all the time. And Mommy calls you names behind your back."

Peterson's throat tightened. He pulled his daughter close, held her small, warm head in the palm of his hand. He brushed his fingers through her hair. "Mommy and Daddy are going through a rough patch of road," he told her. "But it doesn't mean we don't love each other, or that we're getting a divorce. Adults sometimes argue and disagree, sometimes say things they don't mean."

"I don't like it," she said, face pressed against his shirt.

"Neither do I," he said, slowly shaking his head.

—

Two weeks earlier, in the middle of a big, blow-out argument, Lori had stormed out of the house and driven away. She sometimes did that—just walked off, mid-sentence, without explanation. Peterson stood around for several minutes, thinking she might return. When she didn't, he sat in the yellow chair in the den and watched the growing darkness swallow the room, rising only to pour another drink, or to try Lori's cell phone, which she wasn't answering. Rachel, who always retreated to her bedroom and shut the door when the yelling began, found him an hour later, sitting in darkness. Without a word, she crawled into his lap. They sat like that for some time. Finally, she asked where her mother was.

"I don't know," Peterson whispered.

"When will she be back?"

"I don't know."

"Why is Mommy mad?"

"Sweetheart," he said. Then he asked if she was hungry. He made her macaroni and cheese, but did not eat any himself. He put his daughter to bed early, tucking her in. He had difficulty reading bedtime stories. His speech was slurred. After he turned out the lights, he kissed her and returned to his chair in the family room. He heard Rachel weeping quietly for several minutes, then she fell silent.

As the night wore on Peterson could not sit still. He paced up and down the hallways, into and out of the darkened bedrooms of his house, cradling his bourbon glass, thinking over unfinished business. There were arguments to be made, positions to be asserted, explanations to be demanded. He spoke at length to the bathroom mirror.

The next morning, Rachel went to a friend's house for a play date. Peterson graded papers for an hour, though he found it difficult to concentrate. He poured his first bourbon at ten o'clock and gave up on grading. He checked his email: a message from a student who'd stopped by his Friday office hours but found the door locked, and another from the Chair of the Graduate Committee. Peterson had missed an important meeting, denying the committee his vote on the vital question of—

Peterson shut down the computer. In the den, he turned on the television and sank into his recliner. The Giants were playing a day game in Pittsburgh. It was only the second inning, and they were down three runs. They had no pitching. The batters couldn't hit a river barge. Star players sat on the bench, complaining of vague injuries. There was little hope.

Lori arrived home at noon, looking haggard, dressed in yesterday's clothes. Peterson demanded an explanation. She told him she'd gone to a motel on the edge of town to think over why she should ever come back to their house.

"I guess you found a reason."

"I didn't want my daughter to worry."

"Too late. Any other reasons?"

She shrugged her shoulders. Their eyes searched each other's faces for something Peterson felt sure neither of them fully understood.

She said, "You've become someone I despise."

Peterson swallowed. "Is he really any better?"

"Who."

"Whoever you were with."

"I was alone."

"Then you're a liar and a bitch."

She lunged forward awkwardly, tossing out an arm Peterson didn't even try to dodge. The blow caught him squarely on the ear. A white, blinding flash exploded behind his eyes. He reeled, off balance, upsetting a coffee table as he fell. She stood over him, eyes wide, breathing heavily. She was about to cry. Or kick him. From the floor, Peterson smiled and blew a kiss.

"Oh, God!" Lori screamed, then ran off down the hall, slamming the bedroom door behind her.

Peterson stood. A glass ashtray, an heirloom of sorts from Lori's grandmother, had fallen from the overturned table, along with a scattering of mail. He picked up the ashtray and hurled it at the wall, producing a small hole. An easy repair.

After they'd eaten the greasy cheese pizza on crust that tasted like pressed cardboard; after Rachel had downed four glasses of sugary soda; after Peterson had handed her a five dollar bill and told her to blow it on video games and arcade gimcracks; after he'd sat fingering his Leatherman tool in a booth, polishing off his pitcher of gassy, warm beer and watching his daughter cavort gleefully on a weeknight long past her bedtime; after the assistant manager had made the rounds of the dining room, politely announcing that the restaurant would be closing in fifteen minutes, Peterson knew it was finally time to go home.

When he pulled into his driveway, he saw that Lori's Honda was not back yet. She was downtown, drinking with Mike what's-his-name. He checked the clock on the dash of the van: half past ten. Her class had ended an hour ago. Peterson pondered what to do next. He looked at the bag of rat poison on the passenger floorboard. He looked at the empty parking space beside the van. He looked at his daughter, snoring gently in the back seat, her chin drawn down to one shoulder, mouth slightly parted. In her lap she cradled the stuffed rodent in the miner suit.

The motion lights over the garage door flicked off, returning him to darkness.

He would make one phone call. In and out of the house, very quick. No point disturbing Rachel. Lori picked up after three rings. In the background, Peterson heard the burble and din of a crowded bar. He asked how her presentation had gone.

"Fine," she said. "How's Rachel?"

He glanced out the kitchen window, at the van in the driveway. "She's sleeping. Where are you?"

Lori cleared her throat. "I'm out for a drink."

"Where?"

"Downtown."

"With Mike Moron."

"Michael Munro," she said, slowly. "We made a strong presentation together. I've learned a lot from working with him. He's very good. We're having a drink to celebrate, if that's all right."

"Where?"

"Relax, why don't you. We were just talking. Michael's finishing his MBA and then he's moving to the Bay Area. He says he's outgrown the Valley. It's too small for him. Too many people with small minds, small ambitions."

Peterson pressed a hand against his forehead. "Just come home now, honey."

"He says no one in business goes in for higher ed. It just doesn't pay. Of course, a business prof makes a whole lot more than somebody in the humanities, that's for damn sure. Still, all the best minds are out in the field, working. Achieving things."

Peterson fingered the Leatherman in his pocket, turning it over in his hand. "We have rats," he said.

"What?"

"*Rodentia muridae. Rattus norvegicus.* In the attic. Or didn't you get my message."

Lori was quiet for a moment, then said, "You're drunk. What a surprise. Put yourself to bed, Charlie. Don't wait up."

"Tell me where you are."

Then came the dial tone.

He didn't bother calling back. He took a beer from the fridge. He found the bottle opener on his Leatherman and, struggling, partially pried off the cap. Muttering a curse, he turned the bottle around and tried a new angle. His hand slipped and he sliced his knuckle on the sharp metal. A spot of bright red blood beaded on his finger. On the next try, the cap clattered onto the counter and rolled behind the microwave. Peterson stuck the knuckle in his mouth and sucked the warm, salty blood, surprised that such a tiny wound could hurt so much.

In the ceiling, overhead, he heard the faint tick-tick-tick of clawed feet along a joist in the attic. Then the scratching and gnawing, teeth on wood, an unstoppable urge. It was a strange feeling, knowing your house was infested. Invaded, under siege. You had no choice but to fight back. He paused for a moment, poised between possibilities. He felt his heart darkening; he felt another, other heart hiding in its shadow. He grabbed a second beer out of the fridge and headed back to the van.

He parked in front of the Presbyterian Church on First Street. He left Rachel sleeping in the locked van and stepped into the downtown city streets, damp with a light drizzle. There was a stiff breeze—a cold front pushing through, with the promise of heavier rains to follow. Overhead, tree limbs swayed indifferently.

He dashed across the street to peer into the windows of a Tex-Mex joint. Patrons filled the dining room. Peterson pressed his face up to the window, breath steaming on the glass. He cupped his hands around his eyes. It was hard to see. Someone tapped on the window: a kid in a black ball cap. He made a shooing motion with his hand. His date, hunched over her margarita, giggled.

Peterson stepped into the restaurant. The hostess looked up from her podium with a wide, lipstick grin. "Just one tonight?" Ignoring her, Peterson walked a few steps into the restaurant side, then around to the bar. Convinced that Lori was not there, he threw open the front door and ran halfway down the block to a wine bar. Around the corner, he poked into a Hawaiian grill, then an Irish pub. By the time he returned to the van, he'd been gone for twenty minutes. He was sure that Rachel had woken, found herself locked in the vehicle, alone, and was crying hysterically. But, no, she hadn't moved a bit, still safely snoring away.

The drizzle gave way to light rain. Peterson stood beside his van in the street, nibbling anxiously at a hangnail. Rain dampened his shirt. His feet were wet and cold: he wore sandals with no socks. He peered in the window at his sleeping daughter. He ran his fingers over the front of his jeans, feeling for his car keys.

In the van, he opened his second beer. He drove slowly through the maze of downtown streets. He circled City Plaza, muttering rationalizations. His eyes scanned the curbsides and parking lots, searching for Lori's Honda. He followed Fifth Street out of downtown, into the student ghetto of banner-clad fraternity houses, decrepit Victorians, and cinderblock apartment units. Cars were parked on front lawns. Music throbbed from bedroom windows. He turned left, right, left again. He wasn't sure where he was. The city blocks suddenly looked identical, each turn folding back onto itself. Young people were everywhere: stumbling along sidewalks; clustered on porches, steps, and driveways; smoking cigarettes and laughing; leaning against parked cars; guzzling greedily from red plastic cups. Drunkards, every last one. His people.

A girl in a short skirt stepped out from between two parked cars, just feet in front of Peterson's van; he stood on the brake, spilling beer in his lap. The girl, a pretty brunette, turned to look, laughed, and walked on. She was missing a shoe.

A rapid thumping resounded on the side of the van, startling Peterson. Bloated, fleshy faces leered in his driver's side window. "Move it, man! Get outta here!" Then, "I'm pissing on his van!" Peterson's heart raced. He felt desperate and absurd. He turned a corner, pulled to the curb, and lowered his forehead to the steering wheel.

California. Six years ago, the very name had seemed a promise. The land where anything was possible. To a man raised on northern Minnesota's hard winters and taciturnity, the prospect of moving west—west of the Mississippi, west of the Rockies, west of everything—seemed magical. He'd visited the campus on a bright, sunny February day. Temperatures were in the mid-sixties, with a light breeze. He telephoned Lori back in Minneapolis, where it was sleeting. She was eight months pregnant, as big as a whale. And he told her: It's warm here, honey. There are buds on the trees. The foothills are covered in wildflowers, the grass as green as emeralds. It's a paradise.

Lori wept on the phone. Take it, she said. Take the job. Get us out of here.

Somehow, everything had gotten turned around on him. California was supposed to have been a different dream.

It was eleven-thirty when he pulled into the driveway. Lori had not returned. He shoveled Rachel out of the back seat and got her to sit on the toilet before leading her directly to bed. Then he got the folding ladder out of the garage and, climbing into his attic, placed the poison pellets in areas of high traffic. The prospect of having to wait four or five days to see results irked him. He'd done what he needed to do; he'd taken care of the problem. Now he wanted to see results.

In the family room, he drank bourbon and watched the late-night news. He began to nod off. He cracked a window, felt the cool night air move across the floor, swirling around his ankles.

Just after two o'clock, a car pulled up in front of the house. Peterson moved to the window. It was a black car, low and sleek. Foreign. It sat at the foot of the driveway but no one got out. Peterson left the window and sat in a kitchen chair, facing the front entryway, and waited. After several minutes, the car door opened and he heard his wife bidding someone good-night, and thanks for everything. The front door swung open and she stumbled in, carrying her high heels, which she dropped noisily to the floor. Her fingers fumbled at the bolt as she locked the door behind her.

"I told you not to wait up."

Peterson saw that the zipper of her skirt was misaligned. "I'm not even going to ask where you've been."

"Good. Because I wouldn't tell you." She took an uneven step forward, then stopped. Peterson watched as she looked down at the floor, eyes squinting as if she were having trouble focusing. She leaned a shoulder against the wall and closed her eyes. "He wants me to leave you."

Peterson moved toward her. He sniffed at her neck and along her hair. He ran his fingers along the back of her neck, gently, at first. Then he began to press and dig into the skin and muscle there.

"Don't," she said, wincing. "That hurts."

"I know," he said. "I'm going to hurt you now."

He pressed his body against her, moving his hands roughly up and down her body, caressing and kneading and pinching. He shoved her into the living room and forced her down to the carpet. She lay there, arms at her sides, looking at him. She did not stop him as he roughly unbuttoned her blouse. She did not stop him as he yanked at her skirt. And she did not stop him as he stood over her and stripped off his jeans. She lay on the floor, her blouse spread open like wrinkled wings, her skirt wrapped around one ankle, staring at him with cold, steady eyes.

"Go ahead," she said, in low, hard voice. "You think it makes you a man."

He proceeded, twice dark and alone.

OBJECT LESSONS
or
What to Expect When You're Expecting: How to Overcome Fear of Your Total Inexperience and Prepare for the Biggest Thing You've Never Done

The Stinging Begins

When Julie tells me she's pregnant, the first thing I do is explode out the kitchen door onto the front lawn, yelping like a caveman. A caveman without his glasses, that is. I trip on something, maybe a sprinkler head, and careen into a rose bush. Extrication requires some delicacy. Julie stands in the doorway, laughing. I hold up an arm covered in tiny, bright beads of blood: little crimson dragons, already puffing themselves up.

As I walk into the house, the first thing I see is a crisp new head of Boston lettuce sitting in a blue glass bowl, an image so elegant I nearly weep with joy. Then the stinging in my arm begins.

In the bathroom, I clean the cuts with hydrogen peroxide, small symphony of pain. I tell myself I am going to be a parent, a father. I am going to have a child. The man I see in the mirror does not appear ready. Bandages cover his arms in a haphazard pattern, like ancient, unintelligible runes.

Male Enhancement

We shop at Babies-R-Us, Baby Gap, and the kids' section of department stores like Sears and Target: territories screaming potential, heretofore undiscovered, boundless in their gleaming newness . . . which can't possibly be true because I've shopped in them for years—Target charge card holder since '97, thank you. Shopping in the twenty-first century involves distinguishing various operating frequencies layered palimpsestically atop one another. There isn't one Target; there are Targets within Targets. It's a question of adjusting your receiver. A single guy—or a guy, like me, married without offspring—walks by the kids' stuff without noticing it for one second. The baby aisles are just that wee fiefdom you pass before entering the kingdom of men's summer wear, which is where the action really is. Yes, we're talking about male enhancement: a good pair of summer shorts on sale, with a knit cotton polo shirt, perhaps a rich burgundy.

I don't know which I prefer: the moment the cash register rings, or the moment after.

Our Dumb Century

I want to talk about sex—but not how you're thinking. I want to talk about simply *having* a sex life, which is something I am told goes away after Baby shows up. This strikes me as a bad situation. Because I like to make love to my wife. She is a comely person, and wise in the ways of the flesh. We enjoy sex, and we enjoy a lot of it. It's a point of pride between us that we've made love in every room of our house. (She'd kill me if she knew I was saying this.) We've also made love at literally every hour of the day. I would like to say that I've made love in every room of my house at every hour of the day, and that is certainly an attainable goal, given my wife's generous libido and my unceasing interest in the newness of our sexual encounters, but, alack and alas, this is not the case. Nevertheless, we have surprised each other with our ploys, interrupted one another in the midst of myriad activities, set aside countless other things that really, really needed doing just so we could enjoy spontaneous sexual congress. This really is my favorite thing, more than shopping. (I have fantasies about shopping and sex, involving a dressing room and mirrors, but let's save that for another day.)

It is a fact universally acknowledged that having kids completely screws up a married couple's dynamic. This frightens me. You become, what, robot serfs irrevocably indentured to this demanding little tyrant, with his/her endless needs: to be fed and burped, to have diapers changed, to be watched at all moments of the day, to have clean clothes, etc. Oh, and love. You have to love it, this child. Because it is your own. Because you made it. There is no return policy.

In bed one evening, I confess these fears and worries to my wife. Julie wears a silk negligee and flips through the latest *Harper's*. Her brunette locks hang suggestively about her shoulders. It seems to me that, since she has become pregnant, a certain glow radiates around her, an aura I find terribly intoxicating. I stroke her forearm, signaling my hopes and intentions. Julie turns the pages of her magazine with a practiced nonchalance. It's our little game; I have to warm her up, stroking and touching. I begin to kiss her—lightly at first, on the backs of her hands, on her upper arms, her neck. My hand slips between her thighs. Ordinarily, this is when the light gets switched off and things become more interesting, but tonight she puts a hand against my chest and gives me a gentle push.

I tumble onto my side, defeated. I ask what's wrong.

One of those long and, yes, pregnant pauses ensues, which television has taught us shall be followed by some rare bit of insight.

"When you talk about our child," Julie says, "you sound selfish and self-centered."

"I'm trying," I say. "It's just . . . I like my world the way it is. Is that so bad?"

Julie tells me I've got it all backwards, that the point of parenting is to put the child first. This will be, she assures me, both beautiful and sublime. An opportunity for me, for us, to grow. It will be the pinnacle of our marriage.

Outwardly, I must agree with this. Inwardly, I harbor doubts and insecurities about what will happen to our marriage, about what will happen to me. Marriage! Did you ever notice the "I," that all-important letter in the center of that word?

"You need to be open to change," Julie says. "It's coming, whether you're ready or not. It's going to hit you like a Mack truck."

"If a Mack truck hit me I'd die."

"Being a father will make you more alive."

"I can't imagine a life more robust than the one I already have, darling." This sounds so good to my ear that I resume stroking her thigh, but she swats my hand away like an angry schoolmistress.

"Stop being obtuse. You know what I'm talking about."

"Let's pretend I don't," I say, knowing only one of us will be the pretender in this game. "Explain it to me in one sentence."

With a frustrated sigh, she complies. "Parenting. It's like that old Monty Python routine: expect the unexpected."

I'm sure she means "no one expects the Spanish Inquisition," and I trust parenting isn't the least bit like that! I don't tell my wife she's mixed up a cliché with a pop culture reference. Instead, I tell her that, in a certain sense, I'm not scared at all. Technology is a huge social safety net, when you think about it. Parenting might simply be a question of establishing one's new consumer identity. There is a whole product niche waiting for first-time parents. There are books. There are blogs. Buy a few things on a website, and it starts recommending related items, or showing you what others who bought what you bought are buying.

"That's how people learn parenting today," I conclude. "You occupy a unique demographic, enter a new consumer location. Shopping is the glue that binds it all together. I'm convinced we need a Baby Björn, for instance. The customer ratings for those things go through the roof!"

Julie gives me a long, hard look. Recently, she told me she's grown weary of my irony. Hey, I'd give it up if I thought I could survive without it. Maybe that's what kids are really for: cracking the seal on otherwise airtight defense strategies.

"I'm not talking about shopping," she says.

I tell her I know what she's talking about, and I'm on it. The compiled and handily annotated wisdom of the ages rests at my fingertips. There's a blog for every type of parenting: active-lifestyle parenting, sarcastic parenting, sustainability parenting, trailer park parenting, parenting twins and triplets, raising the liberal or conservative baby, ditto religious/secular. Everything from Rudolf Steiner and Dr. Spock to some blogger named "SnarkyMom38" in San Diego. I read her postings every morning as I munch on my Frosted Flakes.

Julie is quiet for a moment, then says that blogging is an avalanche of banality unequaled in human history.

"That's sort of the point."

"Point-less is more like it. The index of vapidity in our dumb century."

Oh, my wife. She still composes emails as if they were letters.

"What are you talking about?" I counter. "The twentieth century was great, minus a couple of global wars and a litany of genocide. Radio, television, the personal computer, and Madonna. Come on, sweetheart, drop the Luddite bit and join the rest of us in celebrating the triumph of technology."

"Is that your plan as a parent? To surround our child with gizmos?"

"He or she will be technologically literate from an early age, yes. That is a responsible parenting strategy, in my opinion."

"You don't know the extent of your ignorance."

This seems a self-evident proposition, but I'm not one to challenge the logic of an expecting mother. I've learned that much about parenting! Instead, I ask her to have faith that I can learn whatever I need to learn.

"I hope you do," she says, soberly. "I just wish you'd quit trying to make a joke out of it. Parenting isn't something you study or buy. It's something you do, and you have to do it from the heart. Just ask your brother."

My brother: biological father of twins, stepfather to a teenage daughter. He's happily ensconced in the Santa Cruz mountains, with his composting, his organic veggies, his theories of sustainability. He is very green: he smokes about a pound of weed a day.

I'm of another ilk. I was born to live in the suburbs. I grew up prowling the mall. I bought an iPhone on the day of its premier, and I upgrade it whenever possible because I am a true American. There is no looking back. Whatever we lost when we left Gram and Gramps down on the farm (or sent my brother to it), we gained—tenfold!—in the cathedrals of lucre. The shopping mall was the true university of the late twentieth century; today, it is the online bazaar.

These are the best shopping days of your life, but they are fleeting. Buy now.

The first trimester is rough on Julie. She can't keep anything down. If she says she wants oatmeal (and we're out of it, of course), I go and get it. She tries it, then coughs it up. "Maybe with whole milk," she says. I drive to the twenty-four-hour convenience store to get it. But by the time I get home, she doesn't want it. She wants rye bread.

Rye bread?

"Russian rye," she specifies, "toasted, with a thick slab of peanut butter." This entails a trip to the supermarket, deep into the bowels of our tidy, manicured suburb. I drive the lonely, vacant streets bathed in beechen green and shadows numberless, dreaming of English gardens. By the time I return, Julie is asleep. I won't disturb her.

In the morning, she tries the oatmeal and whole milk but tosses it up before heading out the door for work, where she nibbles on soda crackers and sips spring water. I worry about nutrition for our child, as in whether or not s/he is getting any. Julie says she'll eat what she can, when she can.

I check the blogs and confirm that none of this is abnormal. In fact, it could be much worse.

So I cook dinner for one: Spam and eggs on toasted Russian rye, smothered in picante sauce, which I eat whilst watching a mixed martial arts match uninterrupted by the niggling comments of my wife, who finds the sport bestial. This is liberty! But it turns out liberty is boring unless you can flaunt it before someone.

The Useless Empire of Things

In my dream, the baby is crying. Or, rather, inconsolably screaming: the kind of horrific blare that makes any parent cringe. Julie and I take turns trying to comfort him or her, passing the child back and forth. We try everything—a diaper change, a lullaby, a bit of breast feeding. We try the pacifier, the baby rattle, a teething ring. Stereo on, stereo off. Ditto the television. Nothing works. The baby's lament is unceasing.

Get something, Julie orders me.

Get what? I ask.

Just get it! Now! she screams.

I am about to scream back that I don't know what to get, but she is preoccupied with the suffering of our child. I understand it is my role to provide this unnamed thing, whatever it is.

I drive to the mall. The parking lot is empty. Thousands of vacant slots, acres of asphalt, and not one car! I park directly in front of my favorite entrance. Inside the mall, every store is open. The lights are on, the Muzak burbles like so much mental confetti, but there isn't a single person to be found. Not one store clerk behind a cash register, or roaming the aisles. No customers perambulate the manicured walkways thoughtfully designed to suggest a town square. From one anchor store to the next, and all the little shops in between, I can go anywhere. I can pick up anything, and I do. For instance, a gorgeous cardigan sweater. Since no one is around to ring up my sale, I walk out of the store with it under my arm, certain the alarms will blare. But they don't. I grab the new Stephen Colbert hardcover from a book store, and a pair of high-end running shoes from a sports outlet, and, for Julie, a dazzling pair of Mexican silver earrings from one of those little carts punctuating the sidewalks. I am dizzy with delight at my haul. To think I can have it and no one will know!

Then it occurs to me that I have forgotten why I came there in the first place. My baby doesn't need a wool sweater or Stephen Colbert or Mexican earrings. I don't know what s/he needs, but I know it isn't any of this. And while part of me thinks that nothing will be lost by keeping my little horde, it's obvious that nothing will be gained. I drop my haul in a scattered mess and bound out the door to my car. I get in, start it up and drive at top speed across the empty parking lot, ignoring the yellow lines and arrows guiding me this way or that. I must flee this oddly useless empire of things. But as I approach the edge of the lot, I see only endless concrete curbing and beds of perfectly trimmed hedges mulched with wood chips, immaculate and pristine. I circle the mall, searching for an exit, but there is no way out.

Statistically Normal

My younger brother Dennis calls to invite Julie and me to my twin nephews' birthday party the following Saturday at their place near Santa Cruz. He should know I can't make it on a Saturday; I haven't had a Saturday off in years. All right, he says, come down Sunday for dinner. "The boys want an Uncle Simon fix," he says with what sounds like genuine warmth. "Come and wish 'em a happy ninth birthday. Those little guys can't wait to see ya!"

Yippee. My back is still recovering from the last time those sweet hellions descended on our wee abode. The twins thought it'd be funny to hide Uncle Simon's shoes—but only one of each pair, mind you. I couldn't find a matching shoe for two days, and had to go to work the next morning wearing one cross-trainer and one tennis shoe. I hobbled around the showroom floor like I had polio or something. I came home that night cursing their very names, my back tight as a tourniquet.

"So, hey, you ready to be a father or what?" Dennis asks.

"Sort of. I just wish I knew what I was getting myself into."

"You're becoming statistically normal. Eighty-five percent of adults reproduce."

"Sure. Even Pol Pot had a mother. Why doesn't that comfort me?"

"Because you're high-strung," he says. "But parenting can do weird things. Maybe you'll chill out."

"Is that what raising three kids has done to you?"

"It sort of lobotomizes you, yeah."

Great!

I tell him Julie and I will see them on Sunday. But on Sunday morning, Julie is in no shape for two hours in the car. I offer to call and cancel. "I should be here for you," I tell her.

"Go," she says, waving a hand from the bed, a damp washcloth astride her brow. A blue plastic bucket sits bedside. "Your family wants to see you. You can talk to Dennis about being a father."

"You want me taking his advice?"

"I want you to leave me in peace!"

In the back of the Hyundai, I load my presents for the boys: matching sets of kid-sized golf clubs—just the high irons, a putter, and a driver. They'd gone into clearance at the store, and with my employee discount I was able to buy two sets for the price of one. Dennis is no golfer, and I doubt his kids will ever warm to the game, but maybe their Uncle Simon will point them in a new direction. If all else fails, they can lob balls into Monterey Bay.

In the back yard of my brother's house, the twins, Aaron and Clark, desperately chop divots into the lawn, oblivious to the fact that their plastic golf balls do not move. Dennis and I sip organic beer in bottles as he shows me his enormous garden, his composting bins, his recently installed solar water heater. His T-shirt reads "Composting: it's the shit!" I interrupt a terribly interesting chat about drip lines and watering cycles with an abrupt announcement: I do not feel ready to be a father. My own ignorance baffles me. Am I not somehow destined to fail, to do irreparable harm? What exactly are my roles and responsibilities as a parent?

A few yards away, Clark swings and misses his shot, a complete whiff. Frustrated, he tosses his club halfway across the lawn. Dennis shouts, "Hey, damn it! That's no way to treat a birthday present! Go pick that up." Scowling, the boy marches across the lawn and retrieves his club.

Dennis turns to me. "Sorry. What were you saying?"

"I'm not ready to be a parent."

He shrugs his shoulders. "Nobody ever is. But you get used to it."

"How? When?"

He pours the last swallow of his beer over a patch of eggplant. "Don't sweat it, Simon. You learn by the seat of your pants, just like anyone else. It's humbling, I can tell you that."

I ask if there aren't useful guidelines he can pass along, sage advice and handy tips. After raising three kids, hasn't he learned something?

"Yeah. Don't sweat the small stuff. And it's all small stuff."

"That's a cliché."

He belches into his hand. "Clichés are common truths."

"Well, say it a different way. Make it sound snappy and fresh."

"You want it boiled down to a pat theory. But you don't parent by theory. You parent by instinct, by your gut."

This sounds terribly obscure, not to mention intestinal.

In the yard, Clark picks up a divot and tosses it at his brother, hitting him in the back. Aaron stares at the divot for a moment as if dumbstruck, then leaps on his brother, pulling him down. Soon, the twins are rolling around on the ground, jamming dirt into each other's faces.

"Hey, knock it off, you two!" Dennis shouts. "Put those divots back! I paid good money for that sod!" The boys ignore him, giggling as they roll and tumble over one another.

Shaking his head, Dennis turns to me. "You want an object lesson in parenting? There it is."

"Why am I not comforted by this?"

He frowns. "Who said parenting is supposed to be comfortable?" He says that when he married Gina and became a stepfather to Sabrina, he made one mistake after another. He spoke to her as if she were eight, rather than fourteen. He was syrupy and soft, overly permissive. "I wanted to be her pal. But Gina set me straight. 'She needs a father, not a friend,' she told me. So I toughened up."

One day he found Sabrina modeling a miniskirt and a halter top in the hallway mirror. Pretty racy stuff. When he asked what she was doing, she told him she was going into Santa Cruz, to the Boardwalk with her friends. Gina was not home at the time, but Dennis knew Gina would not approve. Dennis did not approve! He ordered her to change her clothes. She refused. Soon they were shouting at each other.

"Kids need to assert themselves," he says. "Wearing sexy clothes is one way. Telling your stepfather to fuck off is another. I understand that. But this was my Tough Love phase. I wanted Sabrina to respect my authority, the usual macho bullshit. And I was genuinely worried. I mean, you were a sixteen-year-old boy once. You know what's on their mind. Not to mention the pervs who hang around that Boardwalk."

"Absolutely," I say, though the first thing that comes to mind when I think of my sixteenth year is the Macarena, a dance I both worshipped and mastered.

Dennis continues, "Anyway, things escalated. Before I knew it, I had her flat on the floor, my hand wrapped around her throat, choking her."

"What?" I do a quick double-take. "You never told me this."

"Of course not. It was bad news, dude." He kneels to pluck a weed from between two tomato plants. "You can imagine how I felt."

"You? What about Sabrina?"

"She got over it pretty quickly. Faster than me, that's for sure. We laugh about it now. What I'm saying is I made some mistakes, Simon. You will, too. Get over this idea that you're supposed to know it already. Be willing to fuck up, and when you do fuck up, admit it. Learn from it." He points with a finger to the far distance. "I want to put apple trees over there next year."

In the yard, Aaron actually connects with his wedge, sending his ball a good six yards. Meanwhile, Clark marches around, twirling his seven iron like a majorette. Dennis yells at him to put the club down, but the boy ignores him. Aaron hastily squares up in front of his ball, eager to repeat his success. Clark marches right behind him, warbling something vaguely resembling a Sousa march on LSD. As Aaron begins his backswing, Dennis booms out "NO!" But he's a split-second too late: Aaron's wedge strikes Clark on the forehead. The boy falls to the ground, limp as a dishrag.

Dennis bolts to his side. In the minute that follows, panic gives way to relief: the club caught Clark just above the eyebrow, but did not break the skin. He'll have a whopper of a headache, but he's going to be all right. Dennis takes him into the house to ice it down, and to check for a concussion. Aaron is left standing in the middle of the yard, an array of golf clubs, plastic balls, and divots strewn about him. He begins to sob, tears streaming down his grubby face. He's so small, this nephew of mine, wounded in a different way. I briefly waver, wondering what I should do, what I can do, but he only has to choke out one more sob before I put all that aside and kneel before him, arms open. Without hesitation, he steps into them, and I embrace him. His hot tears dampen my neck.

"It's all right, Aaron," I assure him. "Clark's okay. It was an accident," and so on. I know words cannot appease what he feels inside. It is something else he needs, and as I hold his trembling body in my arms, I understand I can give it to him, that he can accept it, and that we can do some good between us.

The Changing Dynamics of Marriage

During the first trimester, Julie's bouts of nausea do not lessen. The poor woman is sick nearly every day and fights to drag herself into her office. She's eaten up her sick time, her personal days, and has started taking the occasional day off without pay. Her boss, thank goodness, is very understanding—mother of three, grandmother of five. When Julie comes home from work, she's usually too exhausted to do much around the house. This means the cooking and cleaning have fallen to me. That's fine, that's okay. I'm a modern guy. I can learn!

Not that Julie eats much. In these first months, her staples are crackers, water, and prenatal vitamins. When she can, she chokes down some fruit, sometimes a little yogurt or oatmeal. And endless cups of peppermint tea, for which she's suddenly developed a passion.

When I ask what I can do for her, she tells me to get the baby's room in order. Hey, I tell her, we're six months away. And Boofer will surely be sleeping in a bassinet in our room for a month or two, so what's the rush?

She is gentle but insistent. The room must be ready when the baby is born.

"How ready?" I ask.

"Ready," she says, firmly. "Our baby has a place in this home."

No doubt. But I'm wondering how I can fudge this. You see, the baby's bedroom is currently, well, it's sort of mine. I have my computer in there, and a table set up with my miniature figurines from this fantasy game I used to play—painted orcs and dragons, medieval siege equipment, all in immaculate detail. I know, you wouldn't have figured it. But, hey, we all have these alternate lives. Mine was quite rich. I had a sixteenth-level paladin of neutral-good alignment with a sword named Firebringer, trusted ally of the cloud giant Varl, and . . .

Oh, hell, you don't have to tell me. I know I have to pack that crap up. The other problem is the closet in that room. It's full of clothes—*our* clothes. We put the winter stuff in that closet and keep the summer stuff in the master bedroom, which has surprisingly little closet space for a house built after the Reagan presidency. So where is all that winter attire supposed to go? Sorry, but I'm not too keen on storing my double-breasted wool blazer in a garage, let alone my pinpoint Oxfords. I'm nervous about creasing. And rodents.

But Julie is firm. She says we'll store the hanging clothes in garment bags. Sweaters and the like can go in sealed plastic storage containers. She asks me to trust her, to have a little faith, to be flexible. And . . . I want to. I really do want to be all of that. Just not yet.

Birth Plans

At our Tuesday night birthing class, we develop a birth plan: a list of preferences, methods, and atmospheric variables that will, we are told, engender the best possible birth experience. Julie and I work on rhythmic breathing. We develop a personal mantra, a phrase for her to repeat between breaths. It's an empowerment thing. Our mantra is our own creation, like the baby. Julie selects music to be played in the background during early labor: a bit of Andean flute; the sound of ocean waves; some Spanish guitar. Scented candles will help set the mood. I learn a few massage moves, things I can do for Julie between contractions. I will be her birth partner and coach, offering maximum support and encouragement.

There is a sheet I am to hand to the doctor at the hospital. It's a rather long and surprisingly specific list of requests, but then Julie has really been researching this stuff. No epidural or pain killers unless absolutely necessary. No narcotics. She'd rather tear than have an episiotomy. There's stuff on there I didn't even know we were considering, like opting for erythromycin eye treatment instead of the standard silver nitrate. Reading that makes it all seem terribly concrete and precise.

Next week, our instructor tells us, we will practice infant CPR. This kind of "just in case" stuff is nerve-racking. I don't want to think about an emergency. I don't want to think about my baby not breathing, or having an intestinal block. I want a healthy, normal baby. Very healthy! Very normal!

Some Assembly Required

Almost to the day, Julie enters the fourth month feeling exponentially better. Her appetite increases, the nausea vanishes, her sex drive returns. (Hallelujah!) She resumes her customary portion of the housework and cooking, freeing me to do the stuff she asked me to do a month ago, like getting the baby's room together.

Julie researches cribs online. When she has a short list, we go over it in detail, comparing features and costs. We order one and, O happy day, qualify for free express shipping. Voila! Before you can say "enter username and password," a huge box arrives.

Some assembly is required, of course, and that job falls to me. Though I am not exactly handy with the toolbox, the instructions appear idiot-proof. They give you a hex key and various screws, metal parts in carefully labeled bags. I give it all a cursory glance before I begin. How hard can it be? I'm delighted that I will be able to use my electric drill as a power screwdriver, and proceed with Step One, securing four L-shaped mounting brackets in place with the requisite screws. The loud whir of the power tool, the steady rumble in my hand, the sight of a screw sinking into a pre-drilled hole: who knew it could feel so gratifying?

It's only when I can't find the screws for Step Two that I realize I used the wrong parts in Step One and will have to start over. I've also stripped the heads on a couple of the screws, necessitating an unplanned trip to the local hardware store. By then it's time for lunch.

After a fast-food burger with super-sized fries and a diet soda, I return to the task, confident that I can proceed without further error. Yet, I make mistakes at nearly every stage. My anxiety level spikes. I blame the garbled English on the instructions sheet. The accompanying pictures appear to be for a crib other than the one that I bought. There is a toll-free number for help, but by now it is point of pride. I must finish this job alone.

It takes several hours to complete the task. But, by day's end, a new crib stands gleaming in the light of the nursery window. Downstairs, I open a light beer. I earned it. I used a power tool! Which probably means I should pour a shot of bourbon on the side.

I want my son/daughter to see me as a capable guy, a guy who knows his way around a tool box, a guy who can change the oil on his car, free a clogged toilet, or hang a ceiling fan. I have done exactly none of these things, but I resolve to do them all at least once before the baby is born, so that when I do them the second time, in front of him/her, I will look like I know what I am doing. By the time the kid is old enough to figure it out, I should be able to afford hiring qualified professionals, and then I'll be golden.

Make Fewer Errors

As we enter the third trimester, Julie's belly swells with radiant glory. Unfortunately, so do her ankles, feet, wrists and hands. She experiences intermittent tingling in her exterior limbs, like her leg or arm has fallen asleep. She can't find a comfortable sleeping position. Walking becomes a chore. She constantly feels like she has to pee. Her appetite is strong, but she seems moodier, testier.

Our sex life drops off the radar again. My chore quotient spikes. Surely these data are connected.

Julie orders a pine armoire from Ikea, which is delivered to our front door. And guess what? Some assembly required. This task proves even more laborious than the crib, but I take my time and make fewer errors. In fact, I'm rather proud of myself after this job, and it becomes something close to a pleasure to empty out "my" room and stock the newly-constructed armoire with coats, sweaters, and wool trousers.

Next, Julie decides the nursery must have alternating walls of avocado green and burnt orange. I'm worried she's going all Kelly Wearstler on me, but I've learned my place. Never mind that I've never painted anything larger than a die-cast miniature dragon (on which I did a bang-up job, thank you). But there's a blog for everything, including the up-and-coming handyperson. On a Sunday morning, I wash the walls and tape off the window sills and floor trim. The first coat is up by dinnertime, and on Monday I give it a second coat. When I show it to Julie that afternoon, she hugs me and says she'll show me the stencils after dinner.

"Stencils?"

"Don't worry, you can do it next weekend. Stars and moons, in daffodil yellow and periwinkle blue." She hugs me again. "I love you, honey. You're doing great!"

Theories of Planned Obsolescence

A week before her due date, Julie begins her maternity leave. In the master bedroom, she has a shoulder bag packed with a change of clothes—the stuff she will bring to the hospital. Ever ready, it sits with some import near the bedroom door.

These nights, Julie is early to bed. She is exhausted with the baby. I am restless. I have a hard time falling asleep. I stay up to watch a familiar late night television show, except that now it has a new host, a new set, and a new house band. None of it pleases me. I wonder why everything must change, why we trick ourselves into believing that change is good. I know it's tied to capitalism, to the need to create desire for new products, to theories of planned obsolescence—the stuff my brother rails about. Such things have never bothered me before, but they bother me now.

I flick the channels: infomercials, sitcom reruns, European soccer. A couple of light beers later, I turn off the television. It seems a sterile, boring wasteland.

What's wrong with me? Can fatherhood change a man so quickly? But I'm not yet a father; I'm an expecting father, a parent-in-waiting, waiting for life as he knows it to crumble and collapse at his feet, and for the new empire to arise.

The Impenetrable Enigma of Change

Boofer's due date comes and goes quietly. Each day now brings with it the possibility of arrival, a word laden with so many meanings that, like Melville's whale, it is nearly inscrutable. In order to reconfigure the borders of one's life, one must accept the impenetrable enigma of change. This will be, yes, the beginning of a new and, I trust, better life with Baby. Only I'm secretly convinced that I will commit countless errors, irrevocably scarring my child in infancy, wounds from which the both of us shall never recover.

When I tell this to Julie, she laughs. Did I not survive my childhood? she asks.

"It depends on what you mean by survive," I say. "I found childhood confusing."

"You find adulthood confusing," she says. "But it's of your own making. You create dilemmas where others celebrate mystery and adventure."

"Missing the due date makes me nervous."

"A baby is not a UPS package," she says, sorting through a pile of clothes that her co-workers have given her: bibs and onesies, knit caps and booties, blankets and T-shirts, all impossibly small.

Julie places a hand on her belly. "Oh, that was a big kick," she says. "Come feel this."

I put my hand on her large, round belly, which is taut and firm with its treasure. A gentle ripple passes beneath my hand, like a wooden block being moved beneath a thick blanket. Then, quite suddenly, there's a quick, dull thwack.

"Did you feel that?" she asks. Her face is flushed and slightly puffy. She has dark circles under her eyes from her fitful sleep. I wrap my arms around her and pull her to me, my lovely, breathing wife, large as a cargo ship, carrying our child in a warm darkness that was once our own.

Medical Necessities

At nearly forty-one weeks, the baby is seven days past due. At our last ob/gyn visit, the physician inquired about artificially inducing. Julie holds firm. She doesn't want to induce unless it's medically urgent. If the baby needs to wait a couple of weeks, she can wait. Our doctor is comfortable with waiting forty-two weeks. After that, the baby is post-mature and various complications could result. There are medical options and, in her opinion, we should consider them.

I ask Julie if she'll reconsider.

"We aren't going to need to do that," she says, airily. She sits by the kitchen window, looking out onto the back yard, blanketed just now in scarlet leaves dropped from our maple.

When I ask how she knows this, she smiles. "I just know." She says there are natural ways to induce labor. Walking is one, and so she walks every day, a trip or two around the cul-de-sacs of our neighborhood. Whatever she can manage on her swollen feet. It is said that basil and oregano can help, so I bake a tray of eggplant parmesan, dripping in homemade sauce. She sucks on licorice candy, the real stuff, rich in glycyrrhizin, from a gourmet candy shop in Old Sacramento. One morning, she asks me to scramble her a couple of eggs and to dump in two tablespoons of castor oil. Even under a slop of ketchup, she can barely choke it down.

Soon we are just a couple days shy of forty-two weeks. Julie holds firm in the belief that Boofer will come, and I hope she's right. Because I really don't know what's next if s/he doesn't.

"Have we tried everything?" I ask.

"Just about," she says. "We have an option or two left."

The night before week forty-two, I busy myself with preparations for the stenciling in Baby's room. It's a Saturday evening, nearly eleven o'clock. Julie has gone to bed. Neither of us knows what will happen tomorrow, exactly. In the mean time, working on the room actually soothes me. I can see myself doing more of this kind of thing—spaced out over time, of course, with frequent breaks to stand back and admire my handiwork.

A little after midnight, Julie appears in the doorway with a hand over that glowing, round belly.

"There's one thing we haven't tried," she says. "Come down off that ladder and make love to me."

"But you're not feeling—"

"—Not particularly, but this is a medical necessity." She smiles sweetly. "You're going to help this baby. You're going to help me. Now."

The bedroom is dim and smells of incense. The sheets are pulled back from the bed. Julie slowly unbuttons my cotton shirt, my blue jeans. She removes my eyeglasses, rendering my world a vanilla-scented blur. She brushes her fingers gently down my chest, my abdomen, grabbing my hip as I kiss her on the mouth. I move a hand slowly up her arm, across her shoulder and the nape of her neck. I draw her to me, her warm belly pressing gently against my own.

We move to the bed. Julie positions herself gracefully against the crème sheets. I do my best to be gentle, loving, sensual. This does not feel like ordinary sex—though of course we haven't had ordinary sex in months. I begin to move in the familiar rhythms. After a few minutes, it seems clear that this is uncomfortable for her, and I pause.

"Do you want me to stop?"

"No," she whispers. "It's all right. Just keep doing what you're doing." She closes her eyes and lifts her chin. "This is how it all got started, maybe this is how it will conclude. Go ahead, sweetheart. I love you."

"I love you, too."

I close my eyes and concentrate, letting my hands roam freely over her body, a body I find terrifically exciting in its warmth and largeness and life. I think back to a morning last winter when, in this very bed, we awoke beside one another, the room washed in golden sunshine, and I drew the sheets back to reveal a body more familiar and slender but equally wondrous, Julie's touch sending ripples down my quivering abdomen. I touched her knee, the inside of her thigh. I brought my fingers higher, into the warmth I wanted most. We moved together that morning, excited by the knowledge that this was for real, that we were united and trying, trying,

trying. We touched each other, tongues clashing wet and hot, her fingers digging into my arms, her breath quiet in my ear, those private words we spoke only for each other, words that excite and drive and writhe in my mind. I felt the rising, the slow build and giddy stirrings: the halo of a sun appearing above the ocean horizon at dawn, darkness fading into clear blue, a faultless new day, warm and moist and richly there. I moved in her, and she in me, and together we brought forth, in a surge, this wondrous beauty we now call our own.

WHAT YOU DON'T KNOW

Beau's house was one of my first sales in Chico, a crucial early commission that gave this new realtor ground to stand on. We stayed in touch after that, eventually becoming friends. It was through me that he met Aileen, his wife. Beau joked that he owed me a commission on that sale, too. If so, it was a debt repaid when I met my wife, Julia, through Aileen. Things go like that, in circles, in a small city like Chico.

On a cool June evening, Julia and I sat on the back deck of Beau and Aileen's house, sipping wine and speaking of parenting. We were in line to adopt a child from China. I'd been reading books about that country, I told them, and was trying to learn a bit of Mandarin. I was also reading about how to become a dad, a sort of primer for the uninitiated.

"That tells you something about our generation, doesn't it," Beau said, tapping the table.

"Dave's a modern guy. He's comfortable admitting he doesn't know everything," Julia said, blowing me a kiss.

"And if you forget it, she'll remind you," Aileen added, smiling. She's a winsome woman, someone I've always admired.

"Here's to the ignorance of men," I said, raising my glass.

"What it shows you," Beau said, "is the unintended consequence of the sexual revolution, the women's movement and all of that. We've forgotten things that used to get handed down within the family, like how to be a father or a mother. It's missing information."

"Except when it comes to carrying a baby for nine months," Aileen said.

"Or nursing a child," Julia added.

"I'm not talking about biology," Beau said. "Obviously, that stuff doesn't change." He passed a dish of plump green olives around the table. I took two.

"I don't know," I said. "I read a news story about some guy who had a sex change. He used to be a woman, but now he's a man, legally and all of that, but then he went ahead and got pregnant and had a baby. What about that? Is he the father or the mother?"

"Freak of nature," Aileen said.

"Or just a freak," Julia said. "Either way, he's the parent. Honestly, I don't see the problem with it. A kid needs love, that's all. If a child is loved, she'll be all right, no matter who raises her."

"Fair enough," Beau said. "But don't you think there's something wrong with a society if you have to consult a book about how to become a father? Doesn't that tell you something?" Sitting forward, he drew in his lip and furrowed his brow. I knew that look; I imagined his patients knew it, too, and feared it. Beau's a licensed counselor. He's paid to have opinions, and he's used to people listening.

"I get guys like Dave in my office all the time," he continued. "They're smart, well-educated, into a career. These guys come in, and they're weeping. There's something missing in their lives. There's something they haven't learned, like how to be a parent or a loving husband. Our society has failed to teach them how to become men."

"Oh, I don't know," Julia said. "Remember when the guy from Texas invaded a sovereign nation that hadn't threatened us, killing thousands of innocent people on a whim? Who taught him how to do that?"

"Men," Aileen said. "Julia's right. That stuff goes way back."

"That's Homer," I said. "That's *The Iliad*."

"At least the Trojans kidnapped a pretty lady," Aileen said. "That's cause for war, every time."

Beau laughed. "Very funny. You're all excellent wits."

A piece of bark about the size of my hand landed on the table with a loud thwack. We all jumped a little—I think Julia actually yelped—and then we all looked at each other and laughed. Beau reached forward, picked up the bark, broken now into smaller pieces, and handed it to me. It was thin and brittle, a dull, brownish color. I pressed a thumb into it, and it cracked.

"What kind of tree is that?" Julia asked, craning her neck.

"Sycamore," I said. "It sheds its winter bark in June. That's when you know the heat is coming." I pointed to the line of trees marking Beau's property, the dense canopy of leaves. "These trees were planted when the house was built, around 1912. Whoever put them in knew what he was doing. They're perfectly spaced so the crowns overlap. That's how you get this deep shade. He was planning for a hundred years in the future."

"Now, that's foresight," Beau said, snapping his fingers. "That's knowing what you're doing. I admire the hell out of that, I really do."

It took me a while to get a foot in this market, but I got in. For a time, I did really well. Buyers seemed to be everywhere, and they had plenty of money. Bids came in the minute a listing went up; offers were accepted in twenty-four, thirty-six hours. If a house sat for more than a week, either it'd been overpriced, or it had a major issue, like a bad roof or a faulty septic. I worked seven days a week. I couldn't afford to miss a moment. I had my debts to pay off, sure, but I was building a solid client list, and my secondaries and referrals were starting to go pretty deep.

In '07 the market turned. Houses sat longer. Prices topped out. Interest rates fell. I was not one who believed there was smoke and no fire. The bubble had to burst, and I worked until it did. We all know what happened next. California took the hit a little harder than most places. Suddenly, nobody had money. Banks wouldn't loan to people who, a few months before, would've qualified. A lot of realtors took down the shingle and moved on. Not me. I was into this market and was making a name for myself. I knew it couldn't stay sluggish forever. Chico is an artsy college town in the Sacramento Valley, nestled against the foothills of the Sierra Nevada. Houses will sell here. It's just a matter of time.

What cemented it all—I mean my commitment to stay in Chico—was Aileen introducing me to Julia. I'll never forget the first time I saw her: a beautiful, olive-skinned woman riding a bike in Bidwell Park, her long hair trailing in the breeze. She'd just moved out of the City, which is what everyone around here calls San Francisco. The courtship was brief and hot; we married and started trying for kids. It didn't happen. Eventually, we learned it never would. So we decided to adopt. The paperwork is unbelievable, all the background checks and interviews. They really give you a thorough going-over. Eventually Julia and I got on a waiting list. We wanted a newborn girl, if we could get one. There was a wait of six to nine months, we were told. Then it became a year. It was a time of hope and high anxiety for us, that summer. But we were in it together. We loved each other and we both believed our daughter would come, and that, together, we could work through whatever challenges we faced.

Aileen asked how our house was coming.

"We spent the whole day stripping floors," Julia replied. "Look at my hands."

Julia and I had purchased a Craftsman-style home a few months ago, a lovely old place in need of some serious work. But Julia was willing, and I knew how to do all that stuff. It was great working side-by-side with her, sharing the experience.

Beau asked me what I was learning in that book on parenting. I told him I'd just started. No matter what he thought of it, I stood by the concept. I was a single child growing up, I told him. I wasn't raised around small children, never worked as a babysitter. Some time next year, if God and the Chinese willed it, I'd become a father. I had to do something to get ready.

"I'm not knocking you," Beau said. "Truth be told, I probably should've done the same thing. I was forty when I married Aileen. Colin was eleven. What did I know about adolescent boys? I've made my share of mistakes."

Julia said the last time she saw Colin, just a few weeks ago, she'd been amazed at how tall he was, how he was filling out. "He's the spitting image of his dad, don't you think?"

"In looks only," Aileen said, smiling half-heartedly. "I hope that's all Keith gives him."

"Mister Gibson is not a pleasant topic these days," Beau said. "But you knew him, Julia. You know what he's up to?"

Julia shifted her haunches and looked at the center of the table, probably feeling like she'd stepped in something. "I haven't seen him since the divorce went through."

"Well," Beau said, chuckling, "I guess you need an update."

"They don't want to hear this stuff," Aileen said.

"Sure they do. Besides, it's relevant to what we're discussing."

"What's that?"

"Parenting. Or, in Keith's case, just growing up. That guy proves you can be a parent, yet not be an adult."

"That's taking it too far," Aileen said. She turned to us. "Keith's moved back home with his mother. He got laid off last year, his debt caught up with him, the bank foreclosed on his house. It all happened pretty quickly."

"The market's a mess," I said. "I've hardly worked in the last year."

"You're working," Julia said, quickly. "You study the market." She turned to Beau and Aileen. "Dave is taking some classes, looking to expand into commercial real estate."

Aileen nodded. "I suppose you have to, to survive these days. It's been hard for Keith. I've tried to be helpful, to be civil, but it's hard." She sat quietly for a moment, then said, "He's bottoming out, that's all there is to it. Mid-life crisis, if you can have one at thirty-four."

"Can't he go back to work as a photographer?" Julia asked. "I always thought he was so talented. He could have done anything."

"It must be hard for Colin," I said. "How's he taking it?"

Aileen brushed a piece of bark from the table to the deck. "Colin isn't on the best of terms with his dad these days. He refused to see him at all last month. This is his first visit since April."

"The yacht story," Beau said. "Tell them that one. That's a keeper."

"You'll need some more wine before you hear this one," Aileen said, pouring some for herself and Julia. I accepted half a glass, though I knew I shouldn't have, since I was driving.

"Last April," she began, "Keith took Colin boating on Shasta Lake, an overnight thing on a yacht with some friends. Colin comes home Sunday quiet and moody, not his usual self. I ask what's wrong. No answer. I'd expected to hear all these stories about water skiing, or dropping anchor and fishing, or whatever it is you do on a yacht. But he doesn't have a word to say, just goes straight to his room and mopes. Monday, more of the same. Glued to his iPod and his Nintendo DS.

"So I call Keith and ask him what happened on the yacht. He says they had a great time. The boys—there was another boy a little younger than Colin on the boat—they seemed to get along. If they weren't fishing, they were watching the plasma-screen TV, or playing Rock Band on the game center. Now I'm wondering who these people are. Keith does have a few successful friends, lawyers with Beemers and country club memberships and all that. But I know those guys. I don't know this yacht guy. And I'm wondering why Keith is cavorting on a yacht, anyway. Shouldn't he maybe ask this guy for a job? He owes me some alimony, but I haven't made a stink about it."

"A huge error," Beau interjected. "From the point of view of due diligence, if you ever decide to haul his ass into court, which I suspect we're going to have to do, you'll have to account for that."

"It's called pity," Aileen said, gently.

"Pity does not pay the light bill, my dear."

"Anyway," Aileen continued, rolling her eyes, "the beans finally spill. Colin tells me he and this other boy had stayed up late watching DVDs. It's the dead of night and the other boy has conked out, but Colin can't sleep. There's all this noise from the back of the boat. The adults are partying or something. He's going to ask them to pipe down. He makes his way to the rear of the boat, then he hears his father's voice. He sounds angry, or upset. 'Bitch!' he's shouting. 'You like that? You want this thing? Come here and suck on it!' That kind of stuff. Nothing a twelve-year-old should hear, especially from his father's mouth. He opens the door—"

"—And they're having a goddam orgy!" Beau blurted.

Aileen shook her head. "I don't know exactly what Colin saw, and I didn't ask for details. He was pretty shaken, that was clear. So I call Keith and ask him who were these people, and exactly what was he doing on their boat? He plays dumb again, and I just lose it. Does he know, I ask, that his son spied him in a three-way with this 'old pal' and his whore of a wife?"

I reached over and gave Julia's hand a quick squeeze, but she kept her gaze fixed on Aileen.

"To his credit, Keith was just as freaked out as I was. He never in a million years imagined Colin would hear, let alone see, anything. But I'm like, What were you thinking in the first place? Why would you do that with kids on board? You have Colin for two weekends a month. You have all that other time to fuck who you want, when you want, but you wait until you have your son with you?"

"Not a good parenting strategy," I said, trying to lighten the mood. No one laughed.

"He said it hadn't been planned," Aileen continued. "These friends propositioned him, right there on the boat, in the middle of the night. He thought it was safe."

Beau scoffed, "That's Keith for you, thinking with his dick."

"He felt bad about it. By the time we were done arguing, he was crying, begging me to forgive him. He knew he'd screwed up."

"He plays the pity card, which Aileen always accepts," Beau said, in a low voice.

"So that was in April," Aileen concluded. "Colin didn't want to visit Keith at all in May, and we didn't force it. This weekend is their first visit since that trip. I don't know what to do." She sat forward, elbows on the table, a befuddled look on her face. It was the most I'd heard her speak of her ex-husband. I hadn't met the guy, didn't know the first thing about him, really. By the time I met Aileen, she'd been divorced for a year or two. It made sense that Julia would've known him, having been friends with Aileen for so long. But even Julia never really talked about him, not that I would have expected it.

I wondered then about our child, if she'd been born yet, if she was in an orphanage or in her mother's arms. We might never know where she came from, exactly what her circumstances had been. The agency had warned us: sometimes the children are scarred, emotionally wounded. There would be things about her past we'd never know, secret histories, whole chapters in her life that we could only guess at. It drove some adoptive parents nuts, this not-knowing, forever dealing with the consequences of obscure hurts. The child struggled, too, often wrestling with anger and shame, mourning a lost family, a lost place in the world. Even the best adoptive parents sometimes felt shut out, cut off, rejected.

Julia and I had talked it over. We knew these things might be issues, and we felt sure we could handle it. More than that: we were prepared to accept our child as she came to us, because to accept a person for who she is, without judgment, has to be the single greatest act a loving parent can offer. Unqualified, unconditional love: there can be nothing stronger.

On the drive home, Julia daubed at her eyes with a tissue.

"You're crying," I said. "What's wrong?"

"The wine," she said, forcing a little laugh. "That and . . . I'm just torn up about Colin and his dad. I don't know why."

I put a hand on her thigh. "Nothing like that will ever happen to us. You're going to be a terrific mother."

"I don't know," she said, softly. "It seems so hard."

"Hey, come on now," I said. "We're in this together. We're going to be fine."

We talked about Beau's attitude towards Keith—the little messages conveyed by his body language or the tone of his voice. He was jealous, that seemed clear enough. But why? Of what, exactly? It wasn't like Keith posed a threat. Or did he?

"He's charming," Julia said. "He has this charisma. It's hard to describe. But when you're with him, you want to be near him. You want to be close. He has that ability."

"Sounds like you had a little crush," I said, half-joking. "Did you?"

"A crush," she said in a flat voice I couldn't quite pin down. It might have been ironic, or it might have been a confession. I wasn't sure.

"How well did you know him?"

"I knew him the whole time he was married to Aileen. Eight years."

"Right. But how *well* did you know him," I repeated. When she didn't reply, I said, "Was there anything going on?"

"Dave," she said, sharply.

There was something there, I felt sure of it. And as I drove home, taking dimly-lit back streets because I knew I shouldn't be driving at all, I wanted to know what it was, how far it went—that is, if it went anywhere at all. Probably it was nothing. A woman can have a crush on her best friend's husband. Maybe he has a crush on her. Maybe they flirt a little. That stuff happens.

When we got home, I asked again. Finally, Julia took out some pictures. Black-and-white shots, artsy poses. Julia in some sort of studio, stretched out on a divan, with a white sheet up in the background. She's nude. She looks younger, with soft, girlish features. Her brown hair is cut in a boyish mop, like I'd seen in her photos from college. The pictures were tasteful, nothing to be ashamed of. I looked at them, then looked at my wife.

"Keith took those," she said.

"Okay." I asked when they were taken, and she said ten or eleven years ago. Keith and Aileen were married then, she added. Colin was probably two.

"So you took some art shots, or something," I said. "So you posed nude for this guy, your friend's husband. That's not so bad."

She had a terrible, washed-out look on her face. There were some other shots, she said. Stuff she wasn't sure she could show me.

A cold feeling sank deep in my gut. I wanted to see these other photos, but not until we were both ready to see them. "So, you slept with him," I said, slowly. "And Aileen doesn't know."

She chewed her lower lip. "Dave, I'm sorry. I should have told you."

I sat down in a chair. Across the room, new wainscoting covered part of the wall. Julia and I had done that together a few weeks ago, one small part of the larger restoration we'd planned for this old house of ours.

"I don't expect you to tell me about every one-night stand you've ever had," I said, quietly. "I certainly spared you those details. We've covered all the major stuff, right? The important ones, the ones that mattered."

Julia rubbed a hand up and down one arm, as if chilled. "This is going to be hard to say."

"Hard," I said, trying to sound calm. "Because you had an affair with a married man, an on-again, off-again thing with the husband of your best friend."

"Dave," she said.

"It lasted, what, a little while? Not too long. One of you broke it off. Probably him. He broke your heart?"

Julia trembled, her eyes brimming with tears. "Dave," she said, faltering, her voice thick and wet. "Don't be angry with me."

As I listened to her choking back her sobs, struggling to maintain her composure, my shoulders stiffened. I'd been both frank and honest with her, and had never thought she'd been anything short of that with me. We were, in many ways, still new to one another, but that had always seemed exciting. It had never hurt before.

"What is it, Julia? You have something you want to tell me, so just tell me."

She threw herself into a corner of the couch, dislodging a pillow, which tumbled to the floor. I kicked at it, sending it across the room.

"You loved him? How far does this go? Be honest with me."

She shook her head slowly, her cheeks wet with tears. "Definitely not honest."

All of this had been years ago, years before I'd moved to California, years before I'd met Julia. In that sense, she was already forgiven, this woman I loved. But first we would cross this new territory, some place neither of us had charted out. How far we had to go, I could only guess.

THE STUDENT

Howard Baxter paced his narrow dorm room wearing only a pair of dirty sweatpants. Frigid winter air licked his ankles. The window over his bed had been cracked since dawn, and his bare feet now ached on the chilly floor tiles. He welcomed this discomfort, as he welcomed the gooseflesh on his exposed arms and torso, his erect nipples. He'd hoped these things would dispel the thickness in his head. In an effort to instill discipline, to finally get serious about his exams, he'd forced himself to endure an all-nighter, cramming at his narrow desk, reviewing lecture notes on American literature.

It hadn't worked. He woke at five o'clock that morning, cheek resting against *The Norton Anthology of American Literature*, Volume Two. He'd drooled on the final page of Howells's "Editha."

So, the cold treatment. The pinching yourself. The damp, icy wash cloth across the bare shoulders.

He stopped in the middle of the floor and did a series of deep knee bends, then ran in place for half a minute. The coffee machine in the corner gurgled contentedly, full again. He muttered to himself: The Burial of the Dead; The Fire Sermon; Death by Water; What the Thunder Said. He thought for a moment. He walked over to the desk and hastily flipped through the onion-skin pages.

A Game of Chess.

"God damn it!" he snapped, slapping at the thick book. Sometimes he wanted to hurl it out the window.

He took a deep breath, brought things back to the center. He poured a tall cup of coffee and set it in a patch of sunlight on his desk. Steam rose in lazy tendrils. His stomach grumbled. He'd vowed to skip breakfast, to work until noon. A little hunger was a good thing, he thought. He wanted to be hungry.

A sudden staccato burst of raps at his door startled him.

"Howard?"

The voice was sharp, strong. Female. He recognized it instantly. He closed his eyes. It occurred to him that he could simply not respond. He could stand still and wait until she left. Cowardly, but he accepted that about himself. Sometimes.

"Howard, are you in there? Open up."

He pulled on a T-shirt, then stepped to the door. He swung it open to find her leaning in his doorjamb, her long blonde hair pulled tightly behind her ears. A tense smile ghosted across her pale lips. She was breathing heavily, as if she'd walked the ten flights of stairs to reach his room.

"Jennifer Strickland," he said.

Without a word she stepped past him into the center of his room. Her tennis shoes were wet with snow and left small puddles on the floor.

He closed the door behind her with a soft click. "I just made some coffee," he said. "Would you like a cup?"

She shook her head. "Don't you answer your phone? I tried calling."

"I unplugged it," he said. He spun his desk chair around and offered it to her. "Too many interruptions." He quickly drew the bedsheets up, covering the books and note pads he'd strewn across the mattress. He took her coat and placed it at the foot of his bed. She wore a fuzzy turtleneck sweater and faded blue jeans. Color had risen in her round cheeks. She looked good, he thought. Especially for nine in the morning.

"Tea?" he offered. "I have herbal tea."

"That's all right," she said, sitting in the chair. He watched as she picked at a stray thread on her jeans. A small tear was visible at the knee. "You were working?"

"Studying," he said. "Or trying."

"Huh," she said without looking at him. "You have a test already?"

"Prelims."

She frowned and shook her head. A strand of hair broke from behind her ear, brushing gently across her cheek. He noticed she wore no make-up.

"Preliminary exams. To qualify for my doctorate. I take them in a couple of weeks." He glanced at the calendar on the opposite wall with its glossy shot of the Purdue football team. "I should've taken them last summer, but I missed the deadline. I'm running a little behind." He watched her eyes drift to the corner of the room as he spoke. Not unlike his adviser, who had called him in for a conference the week before, pointing out the string of incomplete courses, the below-average student evaluations, the missed thesis deadlines. As Howard mounted his defense, his adviser's narrow face had darkened. There was a limit to the amount of rope they would throw you, Howard knew that. He just didn't know how much or how little he had left.

"Listen, Jen. I'm sorry I didn't call you."

She closed her eyes and shook her head. "That's not what I'm here for."

"No?"

She shifted her weight on the chair. She made a fist and bounced it on her knee. "I'm ten days late."

"You're late," he repeated, softly, drawing a long breath. "Are you sure . . ."

"What," she snapped, "that it's yours? If there's one thing I know, it's whose it is."

He cleared his throat. "I meant to ask if you'd taken a pregnancy test."

She sniffled, then shook her head.

"Just as a precaution. To be certain."

"I'm ten days late. That's certain, isn't it?"

"Sure," he said, quickly. "I guess so." He sat forward on the bed, elbows on knees, pressing the warmth of his coffee cup tightly between his palms. Her sharp tone disturbed him. He felt that she must not only regret what they'd done—she resented him. She must think him manipulative, or cold. He suddenly regretted the way he looked that morning: unshaven and unshowered, in dirty sweatpants and a stained T-shirt.

"Oh my God," she muttered, rubbing a hand across her brow. "This is so fucked up. I'm only nineteen years old." She shook her head back and forth. "I can't have a baby."

He swallowed. Ten years her senior, he felt he should offer her something. Consolation. Advice. Take charge somehow. "I'll do anything I can to help you out," he said.

She began sobbing then, a burst of great, wet, heaving sobs. Their suddenness and their force startled him. For a long moment he could not think of what to do. He feared she might lose control, become hysterical. He set his coffee on his desk, then moved from the bed to the floor and knelt before her. Tentatively, he put a hand on her knee. He moved it back and forth, slowly. The fabric of her jeans felt thin and soft. They sat like that for several minutes, until she calmed down.

"What do you want to do?"

"I can't have a baby," she repeated.

"So, you're thinking . . ."

"Go on, say it," she said, sharply, her voice thick. "Abortion."

His small electric refrigerator clicked on, its hum soft and steady.

"Is that what you want?"

"No," she said plaintively, as if he'd said something ridiculous. "But it's what I have to do. I'm a sophomore. My parents would fucking kill me if they knew."

"Maybe they would understand."

"No, you don't know them." She wiped at her nose with a finger. "My father would kill me, and then he'd kill you. No joke. Do you have any Kleenex?"

He rose from his knees. He passed her a box of tissues from his chest of drawers. She took two and blew her nose, then dabbed at her eyes. She laughed, a low roll of chuckles that confused Howard.

"I suppose this has happened to you before."

He sat on the edge of the bed. "No, Jen."

"Oh, come on. You fuck your students and then they come crying to you, knocking on your door? You get it all the time."

"No," he repeated, more forcefully. But he was careful not to take it further. That would be up to her. He took a deep breath, then exhaled.

"What do you want me to do?" he asked, as evenly as he could manage.

"I'm getting an abortion." She tossed her balled-up tissue at the waste basket in the corner. It missed, bouncing off the wall and rolling out onto the floor. "It's just a question of getting things arranged."

He understood then what she'd come for. He sat for a moment, trying to gauge his feelings. He felt angry. Yes, angry at this girl sitting in his chair. A girl he hardly knew, when you got right down to it. A girl he'd fucked for two nights. A girl who wouldn't even take a pregnancy test. It's unfair, he thought. The thought of refusing her brushed through his mind—at least until she took a test or two, maybe even a blood test to determine if it was his. Then, when they were sure . . .

But he saw immediately how callous that would be, how it would paint him. He stood and walked to the desk. He took his checkbook from the drawer and flipped open the register to read his balance. He thought he might ask her how much she needed. How much did an abortion cost? Did she know? She should really get a test. He'd pay for that, too. She could do it there, in the dorm, right now. Today. Then they would know.

He looked at her, tried to catch her eyes. Hoping for some final indication, some sense of the truth. And, after a long moment, she did meet his gaze. But she was somewhere far off, even then. Somewhere he knew only she could go. A wave of gooseflesh crested across his neck and shoulders, and he felt the chill of the room. He was wrong, wrong, wrong. He'd never understood the first thing about this girl.

He gave her five hundred dollars—nearly everything he had. His hands trembled as he passed her the check. She took it without looking at it and folded it in her palm. Without a word she stood, took her coat, and stepped toward the door. Her abruptness confused him. He grabbed his room key and followed her to the elevator, feeling angry and vulnerable at the same time. He meant to say something, but stood silently beside her as the numbers over the elevator door slowly lit from one to ten. The door slid open and she entered. She stood with her back against the far wall, staring at him with wet, vacant eyes. Then the door slid shut and he was alone.

Two weeks passed. He thought he might call her and ask how things had gone. He knew she hadn't cashed the check because he'd phoned the bank a couple of times. He'd taken out an emergency student loan to cover his expenses. He wanted to offer her part of that, too, if she needed it. He wanted to be present somehow. Not secondary. Not an afterthought.

He resolved to call her and explain that he was sorry about what had happened. He was sorry he'd been so slow to respond that day in his dorm room. Everything had come as such a shock. So unexpected. It was true she wasn't the first student to find her way into his bed; she was the second.

But he'd never faced a pregnancy.

He did not call. He would not tell her these things, just as he had not told her that he'd appreciated her. Honestly and truly enjoyed her. Enjoyed the serendipitous way they'd fallen in with one another at Harry's Chocolate Shop during that first week of the term. She'd approached him as he stood at the bar, waiting to be served. She wore a tight V-neck sweater. Her warm embrace surprised him, the sudden press of her bosom. The breath of rum and Coke, hot in his ear. She called him Mr. Baxter. Howard, he'd said. You can call me Howard now. He bought her a drink.

She'd been shy later, timid and unsure. She'd wanted the lights off and had worn a football jersey. But she soon warmed and, while atop him, lifted the jersey up and over her head. The sight of her smooth, firm breasts; the dark pools of her nipples; the way her golden hair caught fragments of light from the neon sign outside of her apartment window—he hadn't told her any of this. He hadn't told her she was beautiful.

In early March, he took his preliminary exams: a three-hour written test followed by a seven-day take home essay on Faulkner and the sublime. He panicked on the written exam, spilling out ten handwritten pages and wasting an hour before he realized he'd misread the first question. The take-home had gone better, though he'd turned it in two hours late. Results were due in early April. All that was left now was the waiting.

In the sudden lull that settled over him he felt somber, distant from everything. The studying and the work had given shape and focus to his winter. He'd stopped going out, stopped drinking with his friends. He had thought he would go back to that life after the exams, but he did not. He rolled out of bed three mornings a week to teach his freshman composition class and then sat through his office hours. He quit reading. He left student papers on his desk, unmarked and unread. Spring break was spent mostly in bed, listening to old records from his undergraduate days: Joy Division, the Smiths, Lloyd Cole. He wanted to know if Jen had gotten an abortion. He wanted to know how he could let a nineteen-year-old girl shoulder that burden alone. He wanted to know why he had been angry with her, why he hadn't done something more for her.

But who was he to think he could do anything for her? Who was he?

On the Friday afternoon of the break he found a small pink envelope in his English department mailbox with his name and address written in round cursive letters. The postmark read Crown Point, Indiana. It had been mailed just two days before. He took the envelope down the hall to the grad student lounge and sat in a stiff couch under a window. Outside it was dull and gray, the last dwindling hours of twilight. He opened the envelope. Inside was his uncashed check and a slim yellow Post-It note that read, "A false alarm. Your move . . . J."

He left Heavilon Hall and walked slowly across the quadrangle. He paused in the middle of the wide walkway between the Student Union and Stewart Center to read the note again. "Your move." It baffled him. Was she expecting something from him, some kind of response? Was she taunting him? An icy wind blew down the corridor, chilling his hands. He had left his gloves in his dorm room that morning.

He walked to a nearby bar to get a burger and a glass of beer. He ended up staying for several hours, drinking alone and watching a basketball game on the television in the corner, hoping someone he knew would walk through the door. But no one did.

This town can be such a miserable damn place, he thought.

He left shortly after midnight and walked back to his dorm. In the elevator, he pressed the button for the basement and walked into an empty lounge out front of the darkened cafeteria, which was closed and locked shut. The air smelled musty and stale. A bank of pay phones stood against one wall. He thought he might call Jen. See how she was doing. Acknowledge the fear and the guilt. Hadn't they been through it together, in a way? It would be good to hear her voice again, the voice of someone he'd once known. In a small kind of way, he thought to himself. It seemed he'd only ever known people in a small kind of way, or had only let himself be known in that way. He wasn't sure which it was, or if it might be both. Or neither. Ah, he grumbled to himself, you're not thinking straight. You're drunk.

He got Jen's number from the Student Union operator. He rang and the receiver was immediately filled with thumping rap music.

"Hi!" a loud female voice offered.

He asked for Jen.

"Not here," the voice said, half-shouting. There was a rustling and then a weighty thump. "Dave, give me the beer now," the girl said, her voice distant. Then, close into the mouthpiece, "I dropped the damn phone."

"When will she be back?"

"Next week. She's on break, man."

"But she's coming back."

"I guess. What do you know about it?"

"She went home, to Crown Point?"

"No, she's in Mazatlán. The lucky bitch."

A male voice in the background shouted, "No, Acapulco!"

"Or Dave says Acapulco. Dave is very fucked up right now. But it would be like her to be that way."

"What do you mean?"

"You know, say different things to people. She's obscene! Dave, give me the fucking beer, asshole!"

"I need to talk to her."

"Call next week, okay?" And then the phone disconnected.

He slowly placed the receiver back in its cradle. He sat in a chair in the darkened corner of the lounge, thinking. Weighing things out. He tapped a finger on his knee. It was tough to know what came next. He would have to choose the right language. Offer an explanation, or an argument. A confession—or a riddle? He threw himself back in the chair. Maybe it was time to walk away, to accept the course of events and return to his bland life in his dismal little chamber and forget about this strange girl who played him first one way, and then another. Wasn't everything in its place? The anger, the guilt—evenly distributed. Perhaps he had not failed her after all.

He fingered the check in his pocket. He contemplated tearing it up, but he did not. The more he thought of it, the more Jen's note both irritated and intrigued him. He viewed the return of the check as a kind of betrayal, a minor humiliation. A provocation. And the more he thought of it, the more it nagged him, until finally he understood that he must aim toward whatever was there, guessing the ground, feeling for the atmosphere, a meaning in search of a text.

A door crashed open far down the darkened hall to his left, startling him. A chorus of spirited laughter filled the empty lounge. Some student group, he guessed. Their warm voices bounced along the corridor, so merry and so cheerful that, after several minutes, he felt mysteriously drawn to them. He stood from the chair and, dizzy with the alcohol, put an arm out for the wall. He laughed softly to himself as he cut across the empty lounge. Stepping into the dark hallway, he felt ready for anything.

PARTY LINES

Ann stood before the bathroom mirror, trying to do something with her hair, when the screaming started. Hurrying down the hallway to her son's room, she found Levi curled up on the bed, naked from the waist down. Ken rummaged a meaty hand through a dresser drawer, upsetting the neatly-folded stacks of shirts and shorts.

"He shit his pants again!"

She brushed her husband aside, quickly locating a clean pair of clothes. They debated whether Levi should wear a diaper. The boy had recently been potty trained and was wearing briefs, but he'd been having accidents every day for the past two weeks. Ken was fed up. Ann insisted they must ride it out, he'd get there. "You have to be patient," she said, "you can't keep losing your cool."

"Right, it's all about me," Ken snarled, stomping out of the room. Ann was glad to be rid of him. He got so surly when he'd had a few, and he'd had two or three that afternoon, easy. He kept the beer in a fridge in the garage, and the hard stuff on a shelf in his tool cabinet, like a drunken plumber. The other day she'd opened the garage door and caught him with a whiskey bottle pressed to his lips. Unbelievable.

Levi lay on the bed, cheeks red from screaming. Ann lifted him up, helped him with his clothes.

"Levi, honey, when you feel like you have to go potty, you need to—"

The boy punched his mother in the arm, quick as a cobra.

For a moment, she froze. Then her anger rose, a tightening in the shoulders.

"Look at me," she said. But he would not look her in the eye. She grabbed him by the shoulders and gave him a sharp shake. "That was wrong! Look at me!"

The boy writhed in her arms, growling like an angry gnome. For a moment, she thought of putting him across her knee and paddling his backside, like her own mother had done so many times with her. She wanted to terrify him, to scare him into obedience, if that were possible. Again, she ordered him to apologize. Eyes shut tight, he let loose an ear-piercing shriek.

Ann let him go. He collapsed in a heap on the floor, wailing. There was no point talking to him until he calmed down, so she just left him there on the floor. She didn't know what else to do.

She sat at the kitchen table, plucking dead leaves from a badly withered houseplant. Ken came in from the garage with a beer in his hand. When she looked at him, he barked, "What?" Ann returned the plant to its spot in the window, though she knew it was dying.

In the car, Ken said that Levi needed discipline, not mollycoddling. Firm rules and a swift hand, by God, like he'd had.

"Slow down," Ann said.

There was something wrong with today's kids, he continued. There was too much permissiveness, too little accountability. "Every kid is an angel," he sneered. "There are no 'mistakes,' just 'things you could have done differently.'"

"Ken!"

A traffic light changed from yellow to red. He had to stand on the brakes, the car lurching forward like a carnival ride.

"The damn light changed too quick," he mumbled.

"You shouldn't be driving."

"Oh, sure. Lay into me about that."

But Ann said no more. They'd be at their friends' house in five minutes. Those five minutes could be loud and red-faced, or a quiet stewing, two hands clenching the wheel. She switched on the radio. Neil Young's "Southern Man" filled the silence, a song she ordinarily liked, though its blaring guitar now struck her as menacing and truculent. She switched it off.

At the marriage counselor's office last week, they'd sat across a table from one another. The counselor wanted them to speak honestly, to open a dialogue. They each got two minutes, with no interruptions, to say what they really needed the other person to hear. Ann had tried to be diplomatic, polite. She did not feel loved, not since the affair he'd had with a woman from his firm's branch office in Sacramento. He drank too much, was short-tempered with her and their son. She didn't feel loved, and was having a hard time loving a man who, she felt, did not love or respect her.

"Good," the counselor said, scribbling on a note pad. "Ken?"

He sat, red-faced, his fists balled up on the table-top. "This is bullshit," he snapped.

"Ken, please try."

"Go ahead, Ken."

He sat silently for over a minute. "I'm not sure I want to try anymore," he said, slowly. "I don't know what I'm doing here. I don't know why we're still together, other than for Levi. I worry about him, I love him, no matter what you think. But I don't love you. That's all I have to say."

Ann buried her face in her hands.

Later, at home, he apologized. Maybe he shouldn't have said those things. He was so damn mixed up, that was all. Those counselors didn't help any. They just stirred the pot.

"You can't take it back," she said, "once you've said something like that. You can't take it back. I won't let you."

Liz and Barry lived on the opposite side of town, in a cookie-cutter suburb with perfectly clean curbs, weedless lawns, and immature trees sprinkled about like so many gangly teenagers. Every house was painted one of three pastels: yellow, blue, or coral pink. Shiny new SUVs and mini-vans sat in driveways. Ann wondered if people ever got lost in suburbs like this. You might walk up to the wrong house one day, one that looks just like yours, and step into someone else's life. Someone wearing the same kind of clothes, watching the same TV shows, eating the same take-out food. Maybe no one would notice. Maybe it wouldn't be so bad.

Liz met them at the door in a sleeveless satin blouse, tight jeans, and heels. Liz still had a gorgeous figure, and she knew it. Like any woman proud of her body, she chose the clothes to match. Ann wore black leggings, a baggy lavender blouse, and green Croc sandals. Seeing Liz often made her feel frumpy.

"Hello!" Liz chimed, throwing her arms out to Ken.

"Don't you look delicious," he said, stepping in for a hug. He slipped an arm low around her waist. Liz pecked him on the cheek.

Liz tousled Levi's hair. "Oh, I haven't seen you in ages! Aren't you getting big. Jane is in her room. She's been waiting for you."

Ken and Levi disappeared into the house. Liz and Ann embraced. "I'm glad you came," Liz said.

"Sorry we're late. Levi had a meltdown."

"Well, that happens." Liz looked her up and down. "You've lost weight."

"I wish."

"Something's different. Your hair. What is it?"

Ann shrugged her shoulders. "Nothing's different."

"Well, that's going to change! We're electing a black president!"

She followed Liz into the living room. Barry stepped out from the kitchen. He'd shaved his moustache and beard, leaving a tuft of silver-gray whiskers at his chin.

"So, is our guy going to win or what?" Ken bellowed.

"You all voted?" Barry asked.

"Hell yes! Twice!"

Everyone laughed at that.

"How about a drink," Barry said. In his hand, he cradled a glass of whiskey.

"Thought you'd never ask."

"Annie?"

She asked for a glass of white wine. The television was on with the sound muted. An anchorman sat behind a desk, with a large map of the United States behind him. A few states in the northeast were already blue; two along the south Atlantic were red. The rest of the nation was grey, up for grabs. The polls in California wouldn't close until eight o'clock.

Liz handed Ann a glass of wine. "I really think Obama can win," she said, nodding to the television. "I mean, I'm hoping."

"That's if the Republicans don't steal it again," Barry said. "They're pretty good at that."

"Not this year," Ken said. "They can't steal it from this guy." He stood, feet spread, holding a longneck beer against his plump belly.

"Palin says he's a socialist," Ann said. "Did you hear that?"

"That's a laugh," said Barry. "You want a definition of socialism? How about a three-thousand dollar check from the State of Alaska, handed out to every man, woman and child? I'd like to ask the governor what she calls that."

"The woman knows how to dress," Liz said. "She looks great in heels."

"She's a fine-looking lady," Ken said.

Ann said, "Michelle Obama is good-looking."

"But she's not sexy," Ken said.

"I don't know." Ann folded her arms. "She dresses well. She's smart. She has class."

"All good things, my dear, but they don't spell sexy."

"Your spelling has always been lousy," Ann said.

In the living room, Ann and Ken sat on opposite ends of the couch, an empty cushion between them. Barry and Liz sat next to each other on a loveseat. Liz had her hand on Barry's knee, stroking it softly. Married just nine months, they were still in that lovey-dovey phase, or seemed to be. Ann knew Liz was seeing Doug H., a guy she'd been seeing for years—long before her divorce from her first husband, Steve. Liz had surprised some people when she married Barry, rather than Doug. But Ann understood. Barry had money and a steady job, he wanted to be a stepfather, he was dull and predictable. Liz needed stability so that she had something to resist, something to undermine.

Ann had tried to tell that to her once, and Liz had gotten very angry with her—furious, in fact. Liz turned the tables, accusing Ann of jealousy, of being too spineless to break the rules once in a while. If Ann was so unhappy and bored with her life, it was nobody's fault but her own!

That was years ago, Ann remembered. Long before Ken, back when Ann dated one man after another, never satisfied or found satisfactory. Liz once told her, You expect too much. Love is far from perfect, honey. Lower your standards. Settle for good and maybe good will become great. Hell, a girl is lucky if she can just find good. In the mean time, enjoy the ride.

That's when she fell in love with Ken.

Flashy computer graphics crossed the television screen, punctuated by the ceaseless chatter of the broadcasters. Ann found it annoying. How much was there to talk about? It'd be hours before the results were in. What could these people possibly have to say? And why would you want to listen? Because people want their opinions handed to them, Ann thought. They want someone else to do their thinking for them. Why didn't they talk about *that*?

Ken put his empty beer bottle on the table, and leaned over for some chips.

"You want another beer, Ken?"

"I'm thinking about that whiskey."

"Sure thing," said Barry, heading for the kitchen. "A little ice?"

"Very little."

Ann shot him a look.

"I'll be fine in an hour or two," he said, quietly.

"I'm driving home."

Liz stood and smoothed her jeans. "I'll check on dinner." She walked into the kitchen.

Ken sat forward on the couch. "Don't lay into me here."

"Why do you drink yourself stupid?"

"What's your problem? I'm having a drink with friends. *Your* friends. We're watching the first black man get elected president. You ought to be happy."

"I'm not talking about the election."

"Exactly," Ken said. "You're off the topic, pissing in the bushes again."

She frowned. "I've asked you to stop saying that."

Barry returned with Ken's drink. "Annie, how are you on the wine?"

She held her glass up, still half full. "Okay for now."

"I'm opening a Riesling," Liz said from the kitchen. "It's going to go good with these pork chops."

"We've got the kids set up in the back room with a movie and a pizza," Barry said. "We won't be seeing them for a while."

"Until the piñata," Liz said. "They won't want to miss that."

"The what?" Ken said.

"Liz bought a George Bush piñata," Barry said. "Once a winner has been declared, she wants us to go out back and have at it."

"You're kidding," Ann said.

Ken laughed. "I'll knock the stuffing out of that son of a bitch!"

"There's candy in it," Barry said, "for the kids."

Liz smiled. "Aren't you all excited about this? After eight years of that guy in the White House, it comes down to this. It's pretty exciting."

"A black man wins a state like North Carolina, you know he's crossing party lines," Barry said. "But it's far from over. Anything could happen."

"I'm ready for the campaigning to end," Ann said. "If I hear one more ad from either side, I'm going to be sick."

"I'll have a go at that piñata," Ken said, "yes, sir."

"It's for the kids," Barry said.

A buzzer sounded in the kitchen. Barry went after it. A few minutes later, he passed through the living room with a pizza on a cookie sheet, a big red oven mitt on his hand. On the television, Ann watched as more blue states appeared, and more red. The news anchors predicted that New Mexico would go blue, as would Minnesota. Barry returned, slapping the oven mitt against his thigh. "The kids are doing great," he said. "They're thirty minutes into their movie and now they're stuffing their faces full of cheese pizza. Next up are some pork chops."

"And a new president," Liz said.

"I'll drink to that," Ken said, draining his whiskey.

Barry said there was more liquor in the kitchen, and everyone should just help themselves.

"Don't mind if I do," Ken said, lifting himself from the couch.

Ann decided to check on the kids. She walked down the hallway and opened the door of the play room. Jane sat in front of the television, a half-eaten piece of pizza in her hand. She stared at the screen, transfixed by the tractor-tipping scene from *Cars*. Such a pretty girl, Ann thought. She'll be a heartbreaker, like her mother. And her father. God, she looks just like Steve—the handsome, pointed chin, the widow's peak hairline. So beautiful.

Levi sat alone in the corner, his back to the room, rolling a dump truck back and forth. Ann walked in and crouched down next to him. She rubbed a hand up and down his back.

"Hey, buddy, aren't you going to eat your pizza?"

Levi ignored her, making little truck noises and pushing the toy back and forth.

"You're supposed to be watching the movie and eating your dinner."

It was like she wasn't there at all, like she hadn't said anything, so complete was his lack of attention. He lifted himself up on his hands and knees, scooting the little truck along. That's when she smelled it.

"Levi, did you have an accident?"

She picked him up by the armpits and stood him on his feet. She pulled the waistband of his shorts and underwear back just far enough to confirm what she suspected. Then she grabbed him by the hand and walked to the bathroom. Levi did not put up a fight. He let her strip him bare and wipe his bottom. Then she sat him on the potty and told him to do his business. She would be back in a moment with some clean clothes.

Ann crossed the living room on her way to the front hall to collect her bag. Barry was out back, manning the grill. A thin stream of blue-gray smoke chugged out of the Weber kettle. Ken was yucking it up in the kitchen with Liz, helping himself to the whiskey, no doubt.

Her bag was not in the hall. It must still be in the car, she thought. She walked down the driveway to the curb, where the van sat, unlocked. The bag was on the front seat, right where she'd left it. She stood at the curb, the car door open, bag in hand. There were certain moments in each day when a person was confronted with a choice. Whether to linger for a minute in solitary silence, or return to her son. There were other choices. She might start the car and drive off to Tahoe or Reno. No, if she left, she'd go far. Some place no one would think to look for her. El Paso, Texas. Minneapolis, Minnesota. Woodstock, New York. People did that—walked out of one life and started another, with no plan or focus. Just the will to do it, to leave everything behind. To put yourself first. It was a fantasy of solitude, the illusion of a life without responsibilities. A daydream without men. Men she could live without, for a time. Without her husband, certainly. And perhaps, she could admit privately, without her son.

"I could live without my son."

There, she'd said it. To herself, standing beside a car on a cool November evening, but still. The words had been said.

There'd been two incident write-ups at daycare in the last month: one report of Levi hitting another boy, and another concerning a ball thrown into a girl's face. In each case, Ann had stayed to speak with his teacher, asking for details. The fight with the boy was perfunctory, a squabble over a shared toy. Both parties were equally to blame. More distressing was the ball incident. The children had been out on the playground, a group of them playing soccer. Somebody pushed Levi and he fell; when he got up, he grabbed the soccer ball and threw it directly in the face of a little girl, knocking her down. Of course, Levi was separated. That's when he became hysterical. That was the word the teacher had used. It was odd, she said, because immediately after he'd thrown the ball, he seemed calm. It wasn't until he was disciplined that he became enraged. They hadn't seen that in Levi before. Did he have those kinds of tantrums at home?

A few, Ann said. More in recent weeks than before.

The teacher nodded and reassured her that it was all normal developmental stuff. They'd work on it at school, and she knew Ann was working on it at home. "He'll get the message," she said. "It takes some of them a while, and for some it gets worse before it gets better, but he'll be all right."

Ann re-entered the house and went directly to the bathroom, where she found Levi sitting dutifully on the toilet.

"Mommy, I did it," he said, smiling.

"Honey, that's great!"

Then she knelt beside him and saw the poop on his fingers, the poop smeared up and down his thigh, and all over his backside. He'd pooped in the potty, but then had played with it.

Well, this was new. Of all the crazy, annoying, worrisome things her son had done, he'd never presented himself covered in his own feces. Really, she didn't know what to say. It was one of those moments, like when you drop a glass in the kitchen, and suddenly spilled liquid and shards of glass are everywhere, a terrible mess you wish hadn't happened, and yet it has happened, and there's really nothing to say about it. You can't walk away from it; you just have to clean it up.

And so Ann did. In a quiet, deadpan voice, she told Levi it was filthy and disgusting, that he was never to do this again, that it was unhealthy and that she really, really didn't want to have to wipe poop off her four-year-old son like that ever again. She helped him stand from the toilet, wiped him clean, and then tossed him in the bath. She gave him a quick scrub and a rinse—thank God Liz had Jane's baby shampoo and soap there, and Ann knew where the clean towels were. A few minutes later, she had her son cleaned up. Then she scooted him back into the play room with orders to eat his pizza. He immediately resumed playing with the dump truck in the corner, as if nothing had happened. And maybe, for him, it hadn't. Why was he so withdrawn, so quiet and moody? These moments of quiet detachment were almost more disturbing than his tantrums. Ann feared he was cut off, emotionally distant, unreachable. She'd almost rather have him yell at her. At least then she knew what he was feeling, what he was thinking.

Ann returned to the living room. Barry was still out back, dancing around the Weber like a toreador. Ann looked at the television, but things hadn't changed much. She moved to the kitchen counter. She could use another glass of wine. The bottle stood atop a folded newspaper, droplets of condensation beading like sweat on the green glass. Ken and Liz stood in the far corner of the kitchen, their backs to the room. Ken had his hands on Liz's upper arms, his chin low over her shoulder. He whispered something in her ear; she purred a soft laugh. His hand curled slowly around her waist, out of sight. He planted a kiss on Liz's neck.

A spike of adrenaline coursed through Ann's body, her heart thrumming. She stepped away, around the corner and out of view. She reached a hand out to the wall, the plaster cool and dry.

From the rear patio, the clatter of something metal—a dropped pair of barbeque tongs, followed by a sharp curse. "Liz? Somebody? Come out here," Barry called. "Need some help."

"Got it," Ken said, loudly. He came out of the kitchen, a smile tucked in the corner of his mouth. He stepped around his wife, giving her a cursory glance, as he headed for the patio.

"There you are," Liz said, smiling. She stood at the opposite end of the counter, pouring a glass of white wine. "I opened that Riesling. You ready for a glass?"

Ann couldn't speak. Something felt chopped up inside her, raw.

"Why don't you help me set this table," Liz said, moving to the family room. "I want to show you something."

Ann stood at one end of the table, watching Liz fold napkins and set out silver.

"These plates," Liz told her, "are Colclough bone china. I found them on our last trip to San Francisco. I hadn't been looking for anything. We just stumbled onto the set in a shop. I knew right away I had to have it. Look at this design." She held a plate out for Ann to inspect. The pattern, painted around the outer rim of the plate, was of a large scarlet rose on the stem, placed beside a smaller lavender rose. Both flowers were angled off to one side, aligned in the same direction, so that it appeared as if the smaller rose had turned away from the larger rose, would not speak to it or acknowledge it. Yet the larger rose pursued it.

"Isn't it beautiful?" Liz asked. "I positively *stole* it. The guy didn't know what he had. I've seen this pattern on eBay for, like, six bucks a plate. Guess what I paid for a complete setting?"

Ann looked up from the plate in her friend's hand, into the cloudy blue-gray of her eyes. "I want to talk to you," she said.

Liz tilted her head to one side, waiting.

The patio door slid open and the men hurried in bearing roast meat and grilled corn on platters. "It's hot, it's ready, let's eat," Barry sang.

They sat within eyeshot of the television screen. The entire upper northeast corridor was blue, as was most of the south Atlantic. Tennessee had gone red. Then it was announced that Pennsylvania would go to Obama.

"I'm starting to feel good about this," Liz said. "That's some serious good news. Pennsylvania could've gone either way, right?"

"There are still some big states up for grabs," Ken said. "Ohio is one. Florida."

Ann carved into her pork chop. The meat was undercooked, bleeding juices onto the plate. She didn't think she could eat.

"Karl Rove is just biding his time," Barry muttered. "His little thieves are slinking around in the alleys. They'll steal this thing yet."

"Rove is out," Liz said.

"He's been out for a while now," Ken added.

"He's not out," Barry said. "He works behind the scenes. He's hiding."

"Lots of people are hiding," Ann said.

"Honey, these chops are fantastic," Liz said. "Pass Ann the wine. She's a little low."

"I'm all right," Ann said. "I'm driving. Someone has to stay sober around here."

"You can have one more," Barry said, leaning over and filling her glass. Ann saw that Ken's whiskey glass had been topped off again.

"We've still got a piñata to whap," Liz said.

"I'm going to enjoy ripping into that bastard, even if it is an effigy," Ken said.

"It's for the kids," Barry said.

"Has anybody checked on the kids?" Liz asked.

"I did," Ann said. "They're fine. Everything is fine."

"How about that Riesling," Liz said. "What do you think?"

"I don't care for it," Ann said. Liz frowned.

"Hang on, here's an update," Barry said, pointing to the television.

On the screen, the Midwest lit up. Illinois and Minnesota were blue, as was Iowa. Texas and Oklahoma were red. In the upper corners of the television screen, a running count of the electoral college votes ticked along. Obama had just over 200, while McCain had 132.

"Two-seventy, that's the magic number," Ken said.

"We'll know in a little bit," Liz said. "It won't be long now. When those big states chime in, we're going to get some good news for a change."

"You all sound like it's a foregone conclusion," Barry said. "You don't remember Al Gore. You don't remember 2000, or '04."

"I remember," Ann said. "They stole it. They cheated."

"Yes!" Barry slapped a palm on the table top, upsetting his dinner roll. "That's exactly what it was!"

Just before eight o'clock the news cut away for a long string of commercials. A few minutes later, when the broadcast resumed, big letters flashed across the screen: BARACK OBAMA ELECTED 44th PRESIDENT OF THE UNITED STATES.

"Oh my god!" Liz yelped. "He did it!"

"Hold on," Barry said, "how'd they figure that?"

Liz and Ken were on their feet, hugging and kissing each other's cheeks. With a shrug of his shoulders, Barry joined them. Ann embraced her husband and friends, then stood off to the side. Liz produced a bag of New Year's toys, and she, Ken and Barry blew on whistles and spun noise makers. Ann held a tin horn in her hand but did not blow into it. Now that the moment was here, now that they knew, she felt both awed and confused, because, really, no one knew what happened next. He might become that rare order of leader, a Lincoln or an FDR. Or he might stagger and fall under the weight of expectations. A lunatic might shoot him. Nobody knew.

The kids, looking sleepy and sated, came out of the den and joined the adults. Levi asked her what was going on. She knelt and hugged her son, kissing the top of his head. Something historic has happened, she told him, something he and his own children would read about in school. A black man has been elected President of the United States.

The other adults danced around like clowns, tooting on horns and clapping. Ann held Levi as he watched, wide-eyed. "I don't understand," he said.

"I don't either." She patted his head—perhaps, she imagined, for the last time.

The polls had closed in most western states. As expected, the entire Pacific coast had gone blue. Nevada and New Mexico were blue, too. It was projected that Obama had won Ohio, and that was enough for the newscasters to call it early. On the television, there were crowd shots in New York City, Atlanta, Philadelphia, and in Grant Park, Chicago. An entire nation was jubilant, cheering. Men and women wept in the street. A collective moment of exaltation and joyous disbelief: *America got it right this time*, they all seemed to say.

For a while, they watched the reporters and news analysts on the television, chattering about what this all meant. As if anyone knew! As if a change this profound, this fundamental could be summed up in a few words by an aging anchorman, or some young gun in a Brooks Brothers suit. No one knew what it meant, Ann felt, not yet. It'd be months, years before anyone knew.

The children returned to the play room. The adults finished their meals and cleared the table. They watched McCain's concession speech, sullied by the outbursts of his boorish tribe. They listened to Obama's stirring acceptance. They drank more wine, and then the whiskey came around.

Barry said he had something special he wanted to share. From his shirt pocket, he produced a fat joint. "I rolled this for the occasion," he said.

The adults moved outside, onto the rear patio. They sat in padded lawn chairs. Barry lit the joint and took a big drag, then he passed it to Liz, who took a quick hit. She passed it to Ann, who hesitated—but what the hell. She puffed lightly. It'd been years since she'd gotten high. She'd smoked in college with Liz and the other girls from the sorority. After that, it became a rare thing, usually just with Liz and Steve.

Ann passed the joint to Ken.

"There's a nice, clear moon up there," he said, before taking a drag.

"First quarter of the Frost moon," Barry said. "The Algonquins called it the Beaver moon. It's when they laid their last traps, before winter hit."

"Frost moon," Ken said, coughing a little. He puffed again on the joint before passing it to Barry.

"Can you believe it?" Liz said. "I mean, can you guys really believe he won?" Barry handed her the joint. She took a drag, then passed it to Ann. Ann shook her head and gave it to Ken.

Ken held the joint up before his lips as he spoke. "I was born in 1966, right in the middle of the Vietnam war. I've been living in darkness ever since."

"Oh, Jesus Christ," Ann spat.

"You guys know what I mean," Ken said.

"The Cold War, civil rights, everything," Liz muttered.

Ken turned to Ann. "That didn't mean what you think it meant."

"You don't know what you mean. It means you're drunk."

"It's all going to change," Liz said. "It's already changing."

They were quiet as the joint made a final round. Ann took a short, light puff. Just a touch, that was all she wanted. She could live without this kind of thing—had lived without it for years. There were a lot of things she could live without, if she really put her mind to it. Willpower and courage, that's all she needed. If anything, tonight seemed a confirmation of that: her nation had the courage to elect a black president, to make a change, something that rewrote history. If a nation of people could come together to do something like that, one person could muster up the guts to make a smaller change.

Ken craned his neck back and said, "The Frost moon."

"Your last chance to do something," Ann said, "before the long freeze hits."

"That's the idea," Barry said. "Hey, is this good pot, or what?"

"This is pretty good pot," Ken said.

"I'm feeling it," Liz said. She turned and put a warm hand on Ann's forearm. "Are you feeling it?"

"I feel something," Ann said.

"I'm definitely feeling it," Liz said. "Just wait a minute, and it'll hit you."

Quite suddenly, Ann thought she might cry. She quickly excused herself and ran to the bathroom. There, she sat on the toilet in the dark, sobbing quietly into a tissue. She remembered a hot summer night ten years ago, when Liz was still married to Steve. Ann had gone over to their little clapboard house in south Chico, near the university. They stayed up late smoking pot and drinking beer. At one point Liz stood up, unsteady on her feet, and declared she'd hit the wall. She kissed Ann good night, and kissed her husband. Ann and Steve looked at each other and smiled. He wore a white V-neck T-shirt, his black hair combed back rakishly. The party was most definitely not over, they agreed. Steve went into the kitchen to get two more cans of beer.

They talked on the couch in the living room for another hour, an intimate talk about Ann's most recent, failed relationship. Steve listened to her attentively, nodding his head. He didn't butt in with *ex post facto* advice, or little criticisms, as Liz would have done. He simply accepted what she said, and she appreciated that. It kept her talking. She kept talking as he slid over on the couch, close to her. She kept talking as he reached his hand up to push a strand of hair behind her ear, as his fingers gently traced the curve of her neck.

When he embraced her, she did not resist. She leaned her head against his shoulder. She was drunk, she was high, she told herself this was an expression of friendship, nothing more. He kissed her brow, her cheek. He spoke her name, his lips close by her ear, his breath hot and moist.

"What are we doing?" she murmured.

"You can feel something the way you want to feel it," he told her. "It can mean what you want it to mean, not what others tell you it means."

He slid a hand between her thighs and asked her a question.

"Yes," she said.

She said yes.

The next morning, Steve cooked omelettes. Liz was bright and happy, reading stories out of the *San Francisco Chronicle* and laughing. Steve carried on as if nothing had happened, but everything felt off to Ann. She tried to laugh along, but it felt phony and cheap. An invisible film separated her from the world. She leafed through the travel section of the paper, lingering over photos of white sand beaches in the Caribbean, wishing desperately she could be there now, far away and alone.

Barry said it was piñata time. He flicked a light switch on the wall and the back yard was illuminated. An effigy of George W. Bush, wearing that smug smile, hung from a tree branch, a noose around its neck.

"Holy shit!" Ken said, laughing.

"Was that in the tree the whole time?" Ann asked. "That's creepy."

"I'll get the kids," Barry said.

"Let me hit the john," Ken said, rising from his chair. "Don't start without me."

The men walked into the house. Liz changed chairs, sitting closer to Ann. She reached over and brushed back the hair on Ann's brow, a slow, gentle caress. "How're you feeling?"

"I don't know," Ann said.

"What did you want to talk about," Liz asked. "Before, in the house?"

Ann looked up at her friend's face, studying the high cheekbones, the angular chin. Here was a face she'd looked into for half her life, here was a friend who knew her as well as anyone—better, perhaps, than anyone. But she did not know all of her, did not know everything she'd done. If this woman were sleeping with her husband, it wouldn't exactly constitute a crime.

Oh, that didn't make any sense. But then nothing did make sense.

"Nothing makes sense," Ann said. "Having nothing."

Liz laughed. "You're stoned, aren't you." She placed the back of her hand on Ann's cheek. Her fingers felt cool and dry.

"I'm sorry," Ann said, finally. It was a start. "I'm so sorry."

Smiling, Liz said, "Don't be. Honey, you're allowed."

The adults stood in a semicircle around the piñata, watching the children. Jane tossed out a couple of broad, looping swings with a plastic hockey stick. When she hit the piñata, it triggered a recording of the president's voice: *Axis of evil . . . Mission accomplished . . . Everyone loves a congressional party . . .* Liz and the men laughed, but Ann didn't find it funny, this mock brutality.

Jane handed the stick to Levi. He moved to the target with startling ferocity, hacking and chopping in quick, angry strokes. Ann felt increasingly disturbed by the ferocious attack, the unrelenting force of the blows, the hot, angry look on her son's face. A child unleashing himself like some kind of animal.

Jane complained. "Daddy, it's my turn again!"

"He's only supposed to take three swings," Liz said.

"Hey, son. Hey now," said Ken. But Levi continued to pound, stick flying around his head in a blur. He grunted and growled, his face red and hot. The piñata danced and flung about, spinning and twirling, the electronic voice garbled and gravelly: *Nuke-u-ler . . . Don't mess with Texas . . .* One arm of the piñata dangled, injured. Gashes covered the body. But it wouldn't give.

"Jesus, your kid hates Bush!" Barry said, laughing.

"He gets like this," Ken said. "He has these tantrums."

"Daddy!" shouted Jane, stomping her foot.

"Get in there," Liz said to Ken, nudging his shoulder. "Stop him. He's freaking out on it."

"I . . . yeah, okay," Ken said, stepping forward cautiously. He made a couple of furtive attempts to grab Levi's arm, but had to dodge the flailing stick, which moved with alarming speed. "Levi, stop!" he bellowed. But Levi didn't stop. Ken crouched, ducking his head, hands outstretched tentatively, but moved no further.

Ann knew she had to do something, to intercede. Waiting on Ken was useless. She stepped forward, into the blue whir, arm outstretched. With a terrific crack, the tip of the hockey stick caught the side of her head. Crying out, she fell, rolling into her son's leg. Mother and son tumbled in a heap.

Liz was there instantly, brushing back the hair over her scalp, examining the wound. She ordered Barry to run for some ice and a towel. "Oh, honey," she said, softly. "What did you do? What did you do?"

Ken stood stupidly, one hand pressed to his brow, mumbling to himself. Levi sat on the grass, not far from Ann, a startled look on his face, as if he'd just been awakened. He stared confusedly around him, eyes bright and wide. Unmoored. Set free.

Barry produced a towel and ice. Liz stanched the blood a little with a paper towel, then had Ann press the ice against her scalp.

"It doesn't look bad," she said, stroking Ann's hair. "Just a surface cut. You'll survive—with a little goose egg, courtesy of your son."

Ken crouched next to Levi, speaking in a low voice.

"It's time for us to go," Ann said. "Ken, I'm leaving."

"Hold on, there's a job to finish," Barry said, pointing to the mangled piñata, covered in gashes and dents. He handed Jane the stick. With one swing across the gut, the piñata separated, spilling its innards onto the grass. Jane pounced on the candy, snapping up confections by the handful. An instant later, Levi was there, too.

Ann's ears began to ring, the pain coming sharper, harder, a throbbing in her skull like some giant drum. She didn't feel high anymore, or drunk. She just felt . . . peculiar. She wanted to be alone. Liz helped her to stand. After steadying herself, she walked out into the yard under her own power. She took deep breaths of the night's new air, fresh and cold in her lungs. Overhead hung a silver sliver of the Frost moon, nestled between billowy, dimly lit clouds. What follows the Frost moon? she wondered. The last moon of the old year, or the first of the new? A night, somewhere close in the future, when one thing ends and another begins.

CRIMINALS

Nestled near the tip of the comma that is the Eastern Caribbean, the island of Carriacou is an isolated place, small and quiet: a land of five thousand people and ten thousand goats. I arrived in May, 1990, wanting only the anonymity of a fresh start. I rented a small bungalow on the windward side, with a splendid view of the Bay à L'Eau, the white cascade of surf crashing against the barrier reef, the endless indigo of the open sea, broken only by a tiny speck, Petite Martinique. Day and night, the fabled trade winds blew onshore, cooling my small house and keeping down the dust and flies. Stray goats nibbled at the brush and grass surrounding my bungalow. Asses brayed in the fields. I ate mangoes and chicken roti, drank Columbian espresso in the morning and chilled gin after noon. I swam along shores lined with sea grape and palm trees, collecting the shells I would later document. All seemed blessed, all seemed wonderful.

All would change, as it must.

On Carriacou, every household collects rain water. My cistern held far more than a bachelor (lifelong and confirmed) could possibly hope to use in a year. But I did not know that then, and so I labored to conserve every drop for fear of running out during the extended dry season. You might imagine my displeasure when I found local laborers freely drawing water from my cistern without my permission. Not one pail here or there, but bucket after bucket! They were mixing concrete for Dutchie's expansive new house, just across the lane.

Dutchie was the neighborhood magnate. His emporium in the village square offered a little of everything: clothes, televisions, frozen chicken, liquor, hardware. All of it contraband. On weekends, the shop bustled with Grenadians, up from the mainland, who'd taken the four-hour "excursion" for some duty-free shopping. So far as I knew, that was the end of it, though there was often the sense that Dutchie traded in more exotic merchandise.

I was a regular at the store, and I was glad enough to see my money plowed back into the local economy via Dutchie's construction project. But I was not happy to have my water stolen. I chased away the first few offenders. When that proved ineffective, I spoke directly with their foreman. He graciously allowed me to fatten his wallet and assured me that the problem was solved.

But the very next day, as I sat at my desk, marveling over a rare find—a six-inch Flame Auger (*Terebra taurinus*), picked up on a recent visit to Belize—I heard the familiar sound of water filling a bucket. After replacing the shell in its foam-lined case, I raced to the back door of my bungalow. A barebacked young man knelt before the spigot, filling a plastic bucket.

I confess, I was struck by him. He had the darkest skin of any islander I'd seen, a rich blackness that seemed to sink in on itself. His muscles were lean and hard, toned to perfection. The fine, angular bones of his face . . . oh, he was a rare specimen.

But foolish rage trumped my wonder. I leaned over the lower half of the Dutch door, shouting about disregard for private property, violated water rights, and stiff penalties to follow. I might have been a bleating goat, for all this fellow cared. He finished filling his bucket and began to haul it across the lane. I scurried after him and, tugging on the handle of the bucket, demanded the return of my water. After a brief struggle, he relented.

I was quite pleased with myself, for I am not, by my nature, a man prone to confrontation. But no sooner had I set the bucket at the base of my cistern than I saw this boy steal, from the domain of a plump hog tied to a nearby tree, a cast-iron slop pot. Rushing across the lane, he threw the pot at me, narrowly missing. He then vanished into the bushes, while the disgruntled hog raced in mad circles around its tree, demanding the return of its lunch, most of which bespattered my shirt.

Trembling, I phoned the police and demanded that a car be dispatched.

Two hours later, Officer Terry arrived, dressed in civilian clothes. He strolled about the worksite, chatting amiably with the laborers, several of whom, I gathered, he counted as friends. At no point did Officer Terry express any shock or outrage; indeed, his only response was a patronizing smile as I hotly narrated my tale. (Thinking back on it now, I was clearly out of step with local custom, which dictates that the police never be called to settle petty disputes.) At my insistence, the officer extracted the name of the thrower: Ignatius Cudjoe, better known as Soup.

Thereafter, the afternoon turned burdensome. First, I was taken to police headquarters in Hillsborough and asked to dictate my version of the event to a poor, cross-eyed girl hunched over an aged Underwood. She pecked away with her index fingers, begging me to speak just one sentence at a time and thereby not outpace her. Next, I waited an hour to see the captain, a flagpole of a man with a West London accent, whose first question concerned my interest in cricket. I confessed total disinterest in all sports. "Quite a shame," he replied, "for we West Indians pride ourselves on our bowlers." He attempted to enlighten me over a cup of tea—served, of course, by our cross-eyed friend, who nearly spilled it in my lap.

In due course, the captain asked me to repeat my account as he double-checked it against the narrative recorded by his typist. Satisfied he had an accurate report, the captain walked me down the lane to the office of the island's only full-time barrister, who emerged from the back room of his dingy, stiflingly hot office in his undershirt. Apparently, we had disrupted his siesta. But when Leopold J. Roberts heard that an American of some distinction was interested in pressing charges against a local boy (earlier, I had proffered my academic credentials to the captain in a vain attempt to command attention), his countenance converted instantaneously. Oh, he all but salivated over himself as he thrust a meaty arm into a stained suit coat. Daubing a white handkerchief against his fleshy face, Roberts glanced at the police report. He assured me we had a most excellent case. He knew the smell of money, if he knew a fig. But, by then, I wanted only a tall glass of iced gin and the cool breeze of Bay à L'Eau. Let the criminals of Carriacou run free, I thought, if it meant suffering the likes of this fool.

I arrived home on the day's last public bus, ruing the lost day of work. Imagine my chagrin to find, sitting in one of my plastic porch chairs, a white-haired man wearing a yellowed dress shirt and a wide, green necktie.

His damson polyester trousers rode a full two inches above scuffed and battered shoes. Clearly, this was an outfit worn only on select occasions: weddings, funerals, and, today, his confrontation with a white man. I confess, there was something disarming in the thought. As I mounted the steps of my home, I felt my anger diminish.

His name was Cornelius Cudjoe, farmer and fisherman by trade, and the father of the slop-pot tosser. Father and son shared the pitch-black skin and muscular frame. But where one had been so sharp and aggressive, the other was gentle and quiet. Entrancing, in his way. I listened to his story: his wife, the boy's mother, disappeared years ago, leaving him to raise his only son alone.

"And he a handful, sir," Cudjoe confessed. "He have the devil in his blood."

"I saw that today. He must learn to control his anger, yes? Perhaps a visit to the court will inspire some reform on his part."

"No, sir," Cudjoe said, sitting forward. That was when I saw the lighter-toned scar that curved from behind his ear down to the base of his neck. An old, deep wound. "I come to ask your forgiveness for me son. He rude and hot tempered, but he all Cudjoe have in this world. We hard-working folk, sir. We ain't have money for lawyer and thing. I go speak with the boy this very night, make him see how he wrong. He will apologize, sir, he will apologize."

Then he reached down beneath his chair and retrieved a brown paper bag. From it, he drew forth a sizeable parrotfish. "I bring you something, sir. Just to show you have a friend and neighbor in Cornelius Cudjoe."

What could I do but accept? I took the fish, felt its cold, slick scales, felt its dead weight. Snorkeling along the subtidal reefs, collecting my molluscan fauna, I had seen such fish; they were remarkable in the sunlight, all vivid blues, yellows and greens. Even I, in my ignorance, understood what it meant for this man to hand it to me. A fish he could very well have sold in the village, or cooked for his own supper. I thanked him, and told him that I would hold off pressing charges.

"But you must speak to him, as you have promised," I said, standing. "Your son is a violent young man and he may one day hurt someone, not to mention himself."

Cudjoe stood and assured me that all would be set to rights. We shook hands. His grip was solid and strong. His hand, leathery with calluses, was warm and dry. His word was good. I would have no more trouble from the laborers.

In the center of Windward sat a small square lined by palm trees and, at its center, the ruined foundation of an ancient, brackish well. In the afternoons the men of the village loitered on shaded benches, sipping beer and speaking of the weather, or whose catch was largest that day. I came to enjoy visiting the square, eavesdropping on the lively banter and repartee of the men. I might even, on the odd day, purchase a cold beer—the only time you would find me drinking the beverage, mind you, but when in Rome!

The square was a lively place. When a fellow passed through, he was greeted warmly by name, asked where he was off to. Invariably, this provoked a humorous quip or comment. No man was overlooked or spared—though Cudjoe, I noticed, proved an exception. This seemed odd, and one day, after Cudjoe had passed silently, I asked the others why he never stopped to chat. A long silence ensued. Finally, an older man, a bleary-eyed drunkard, muttered something in rapid patois—I could not catch the phrase. The men on the benches hissed sharply at the speaker. The old man stood, spat rudely into the dust, and trundled off into a grove of trees to relieve himself.

Dutchie's new mansion was soon completed; he was not one to tolerate slackness. And who moved on to a job in Dutchie's store? None other than Soup. It was always with a mixture of excitement and trepidation that I came upon him there. I recall one occasion, late on a weeknight, when I found him kneeling in a back aisle, stocking a shelf. He wore a tight-fitting, white tanktop. Under the shop lights, his black arms appeared glossy, almost metallic. After hesitating for some moments, studying his figure, I placed a hand on his bare shoulder, feeling the warmth and tightness. When he turned to me, I smiled and asked if he could help me find the corned beef.

"Bakra," he hissed, between tightly pursed lips, "you batty-man." He jerked his shoulder from under my hand and resumed stocking his shelf.

If I did not immediately understand what he had called me, the body language translated well enough. Bakra, I would later learn, is the white oppressor, the slaveholder; a batty-man is he who is fond of the batty, or anus. But not another word on that.

Let the record state that I made an effort to be friendly. Many were the times I passed Soup on the dusty lanes of the village and spoke his name, or called to him from my bench in the village square. Always, I received only his stony silence. Never a cordial word, let alone an apology.

In contrast, the father treated me with respect and gratitude. In time, I would see much of the elder Cudjoe, for he became the groundskeeper of Dutchie's new house. By local standards, this capricious monstrosity was considered a palace: tall and white, with two staircases of poured concrete leading to an elevated patio. Plates of mirrored glass lined three sides of the house, lending it an imperious feel. The grounds were immaculate, featuring elevated rose beds, robust clusters of rhododendron, a small grove of citrus trees, and a garden the size of a tennis court. Dutchie was the only man in our part of the island with a lawn, which Cudjoe watered and trimmed fastidiously. He did it the old-fashioned way, with a cutlass, which is local parlance for "machete." Planting a stout walking stick on the ground for support, he bent over at the waist, feet spread, and drew the cutlass back in a smooth, fluid backstroke, then whipped the blade forward, creating a pleasant, soft song: *schwing-schwing, schwing-schwing.*

Cudjoe often brought me a bag of limes from Dutchie's orchard, or a handful of Scotch Bonnet peppers. His gifts were accompanied by prudent advice: "A quarter lime in a glass of rum would settle the stomach," or, "Mind you go easy with the peppers. They hot, oui?"

I would reward his kindness with a glass of cool water and a demitasse of white rum, poured neat. These visits became, for a time, a regular affair. We sat on my front porch, enjoying the cool breeze. Cudjoe taught me how to play dominoes, as well as various local card games. I showed him my burgeoning collection of shells, which by now included a panoply of tritons, murex, cones, and the like. Much to my delight, he proffered the patois names for many of the shells; this litany of local parlance would eventually become a defining characteristic of my major work, *Seashells of the Caribbean*, now in its third edition.

Oh, those were great, good times.

One afternoon when Cudjoe visited after work, I was sautéing fresh redfish in lemon butter and garlic. He found it amusing that I cooked and cleaned for myself. That was a woman's work. Wouldn't I prefer to hire someone? He could recommend any number of reliable girls. I assured Cudjoe that the domestic was anything but a burden. "To cook is a pleasure," I told him. And, in truth, it was, for I had eaten in dining halls all of my life. I explained to Cudjoe how, as a boy, I'd been shuttled from one boarding school to another, kept as far from my father as his money would allow. I had lived in dormitories since the age of six. As a bachelor at Muhlenberg Academy, I'd lived in the faculty housing for some twenty-three years, with all of my meals prepared (save for Sunday dinner) and a housekeeper to tend to my chambers. Now, here I was, fending for myself!

Cudjoe broke out in the easy, broad grin that never failed to warm my heart. He told me he'd been keeping house for himself and his son for a dozen years, but that, if he could afford it, he would hire a girl the next minute.

"You never gave thought to a second marriage?"

Cudjoe gazed down to his glass of rum. "Some things in life can be endured only one time," he said. "You ain't ever marry, Mr. Carter?"

"I never had the good fortune."

"You doesn't want children?"

"No, I suppose I don't. Ironic, isn't it? A teacher of boys." I gave a short laugh. "But I am, shall we say, comfortable in my bachelorhood?" I hadn't meant it to sound like a question.

"Cudjoe must have family or he could not make it, pure and simple. I wasn't born to live alone."

"Oh, I am not alone," I said. "I embrace *fraternitas*. The brotherhood of men."

Cudjoe stared at me for a long moment.

I sensed he'd mistaken my comment. "Friendship between men, Mr. Cudjoe. The joyful company of brothers, like what we share on these afternoons. No more than that, I assure you."

I filled his glass with rum. "Soup must have a girlfriend, no?"

"He moving with a girl from Bogles Village last year, but I ain't see them together for some time now. Me boy ain't studying the girls. He keeping quiet and working hard."

I asked toward what. I was informed that Soup hoped to move up in the ranks with Dutchie. That sounded promising, I said; Dutchie appeared quite successful. But Cudjoe shook his head. "That what worrying me. Them boys is serious, if you take my meaning. They ain't suffer no fools or skylarks. Is heavy manners they would put you under, if you cross them."

"If you'll forgive my saying so," I said, "it would seem that Soup is not averse to hostile conditions. In fact, he might be said to thrive on them."

"That is my worry," he said. "Soup going to work for Dutchie like a box of matches joining with the dynamite. Something bound to burst."

"Let us hope otherwise," I said, moving a pot from its burner. I invited him to stay for dinner. To my delight, he agreed. I set before him a plate of redfish, rice and peas, and fried plantain. I served a fresh garden salad in a bowl. Cudjoe happily consumed the fish, commenting favorably on its tenderness and flavor. But he picked rather cautiously at his salad with the tip of his fork. Poor man, I thought, unaccustomed to fresh greens—lettuce was infrequently available, and always expensive. Perhaps that was why I had substituted callaloo, a leafy green that looks like spinach. Cudjoe lifted a leaf from his bowl, inspected it, then pushed the bowl forward.

"Is something the matter?"

"You must cook the callaloo, oui? The plant is poisonous."

Perhaps it was the boyish grin on his face, or the liquor we'd had, but I doubted the truth of this. I accused him of joking with me.

"No, sir. You must boil the leaves to extract the poison. You mix it in with peppers and rice, it make a fine stew. But no man does eat it raw."

I studied his face for a moment; his eyes danced about merrily. "Nonsense," I said, calling his bluff.

"Try a bit, and you go see."

I grabbed the corner of a leaf and popped it in my mouth. Within seconds, it was as if a pincushion had exploded there; my tongue swelled and I could barely breathe. It was all I could do to quaff a glass of water. Cudjoe nearly keeled over with laughter.

It was half an hour before I could return to my redfish. The salads, needless to say, were tossed in the compost. I vowed never again to doubt the word of Mr. Cornelius Cudjoe.

In the delicate stillness of the morning, the halls of Muhlenberg Academy had a blissful quiet to them. It had long been my custom to rise at five and to work in my office for two or three blessed hours, before the din ensued. I loved knowing that I was alone in the building, that not a single soul would stir anywhere near me until 7:30, when the faculty arrived in preparation for the first classes.

One October day, however, just past 7:00, I heard the main door open and shut. Displeasure rumbled in my throat. My pen froze in my hand; I listened to the soft tread of shoes in the bare hallway. I knew the footfall of my fellow faculty: the clean squeak of our chemist's Rockport walkers; the slap of the stiff-soled leather loafers of our physicist; the clomping gait of our geologist, who wore Red Wing boots with any outfit—ludicrous sense of fashion, that woman. No, I did not recognize this intruder.

There came a rapping at my door, faint and timid.

Clearing my throat loudly, I bid the guest enter. Young Edward Jesperson stood before me, a student of some promise. He had scored 93 on my first-year biology survey—no mean feat, I assure you. I'd made a note of him to become a mentor in the natural sciences program, to lead study groups and laboratory assignments, and to assist me with my own research. Just three senior boys became mentors, and they often went on to the top science programs in the country. All that would be three years away for Jesperson, but I picked my boys carefully, and planned accordingly.

The only problem was that Jesperson was painfully shy. Asked to deliver a report in class, his cheeks flushed and his hands shook. On paper, or in private conversation, his thoughts were clear and cogent, even eloquent. But in class, he stammered and huffed like an ox. God knows, this alone was cause for ceaseless jeering from the boys. And Jesperson did himself no favors when it came to general deportment. His uniform, all slackened sails, drooped from his large frame.

"Tuck in your shirt, Jesperson," I said, gruffly. "What brings you here at this hour?"

Fumbling at his trousers, he muttered, "I knew you would be alone now, sir. I came to . . . speak with you." He sniffled. His shoulders shook. And then a great, wet heave of a sob. Just one.

I coaxed him to sit down and, though I knew the building to be empty, I closed the door out of respect for his suffering.

"Tell me what is the matter."

Jesperson's tale came, like its teller, slowly and awkwardly. A gang of boys, upperclassmen, had been harassing him. There had been verbal taunts, then roughhousing. His bed was routinely shortsheeted, his laundry misplaced. He was forced to give over portions of his supper to boys who deliberately threw it in the garbage, before his eyes. He feared lights out, and the terrors that followed.

"I've let the boys do things to me. I don't know how to fight back."

His fingers, spread like talons against the chair's armrests, were raw and red, as if he'd gnawed on them.

"Go on," I said softly. "This is what you came to discuss."

"They . . ."

"Yes?"

He absolutely broke down at that moment, a mess of sobs. I have never seen anyone, boy or man, lose his composure so completely. He was absolutely shattered.

I rose and came from behind my desk. I knelt beside him. I took this fragile giant in my arms, lifted him out of that chair, and held him. Let him weep on my shoulder. I told him he was safe now, that he could trust me. It took some time, but eventually he did calm down and recapture his breath. His eyes were bloodshot and lined with dark circles. Every fiber and sinew shook, as if he were held together by so many rubber bands. I was afraid to let go.

The soldiers arrived on a warm October morning. They stood in front of Dutchie's shop, decked out in camouflage and combat boots, holding enormous rifles in the crooks of their arms as if they were out for a Sunday duck shoot. Perhaps they were. Nothing seemed particularly dangerous or worrisome.

A small crowd of villagers huddled in the square across from the shop. I approached the group and asked for the news: This was a routine customs raid from the main island of Grenada, or "Greens."

"Man come up from Greens, he wanting to check on every little thing in the shop," one man observed. "They going shelf by shelf, checking to see if the levy been paid."

"You know Dutchie ain't pay," an elderly matron quipped. She wore a colorful head scarf wrapped tightly around her scalp in the old fashion. "I ain't understand why Government must treat Carriacou people so. You can't stop the smuggling. How they think we going to survive? What else we have?"

"Eh-eh," another man said. "Government ain't for or against the thing. Is money they want. Search must continue until Dutchie pay."

The matron hissed and waved a hand, sharply. "Then I wish Dutchie would go and pay the man. I have me Saturday shopping to do and me husband ain't easy if he not get he rice and salt pork by noon." A chorus of laughter rose from the group.

I, too, hoped for a speedy end to this delay, for I had run low on several provisions, most notably the gin that I poured each day at precisely one o'clock.

It was nearly suppertime when I strolled back through the village, having had my fill of liquor on the palm-shaded patio of The Swimmer's Arm. Soup was being led out of Dutchie's store in handcuffs. The boy was taken across the lot and tossed into a Jeep. The crowd shouted that the wrong man had been arrested. Sensing unrest, an officer barked an order and the soldiers immediately stiffened, their weapons erect. As the Jeep rolled off, several curses were muttered. A child threw a stone after the vehicle.

The next morning, I sat at my examination table, removing coralline deposits from my new acquisitions. This work can be slow and tedious, and one's hand tends to cramp after scraping so ardently with a dental pick. Across the lane, I spied Cudjoe enjoying a leisurely cigarette. I walked to the fence and asked after Soup. Cudjoe shook his head: his son was still in police custody.

"On what charge?"

"Interfering with government business." It seemed that Soup had come between the Customs man and some part of the operation. Words were exchanged, then blows. "Why Dutchie throwing me boy in front of the soldiers, I want to know? If he have something to hide, why he ain't go in there and grab it heself? Is because he know them soldiers looking to arrest he. So he push Soup into the thing, and now is Soup who sitting in jail." Cudjoe shook his head and looked far off, to the water of the bay before us. "He capable of deadly force, Mr. Carter. Serious thing. And he ain't see how this is not he fight. Best keep he mouth shut and get quit of the matter first chance."

Cudjoe's leathered fingers closed tightly around a link of the cyclone fence. "Just now, I going down to Hillsborough to see about getting him out of that jail, Mr. Carter. Just now."

I know it is petty to say so, but I felt the boy had received his just reward.

On the third morning of the customs inspection, I took a bus into Hillsborough, the main town on the island, to buy groceries and gin, for I had no reason to believe that Dutchie would resolve his plight any time soon.

I made a morning of it in Hillsborough. I bought a case of Beefeater's, despite the fact that it was considerably more expensive than at Dutchie's. After lunch—a delightful meal of curried chicken and rice at The Palm Leaf, a rather upscale café aimed at tourists—I made a cursory inspection of the booths at the market, surveying the cowry shell necklaces and the polished crown conches available for purchase. As I stood in the central square, waiting on the bus home, I saw Officer Terry escort Soup from the police station, across the square, down to the government jetty and onto a police launch. Apparently, Soup had assaulted a police officer, needlessly complicating the original charge against him, and was bound for Her Majesty's Prison in St. George's, on the mainland. Once again, I was terribly unmoved.

That evening, as I sat reading a few pages in James's *The Ambassadors*, a novel I re-read every few years for its spirit of life—"Live all you can; it's a mistake not to. Live!"—Cudjoe called from my gate. I invited him in.

He sat on the edge of my sofa, hands folded in his lap. He accepted a glass of rum, though he did not immediately touch it. Soup, he announced rather gravely, was in serious trouble. "He could lock up for years, Mr. Carter. And look at me, eh? I ain't have money and thing. Is how I going to fight this?"

I sat back in my chair, cradling a glass of brandy—my preferred nightcap. I decided it was time to speak frankly. "Forgive me for saying it, but your boy seems rather adept at getting himself into trouble. His father cannot always be expected to rescue him."

"I know Soup ain't easy," Cudjoe said, miserably. "But he ain't have no one but me." He picked up his glass of rum and held it, gently, in his palms. "Mr. Carter, I coming to beg your help in the matter."

"In what regard?"

"I wondering if you could see your way to lend a poor fellow a bit of money, sir, to hire on a lawyer for the case."

I considered these words for a moment before asking if Grenada did not have a system of public defenders.

Cudjoe tossed a hand in the air, as if dismissing a fly. Government lawyers, he informed me, were always slow to act. Leopold Roberts had told him they could force a conclusion in just a week, two at the most.

"Hardly likely," I grumbled. Cudjoe frowned; he believed whatever tripe Roberts had spat out.

I was stymied. Of course, I knew absolutely nothing about the Grenadian legal system, save that their judges wore powdered wigs—delightful! The thought of stepping into Cudjoe's morass had about as much appeal as licking clean the shell of a mollusc. And, I must admit, the thought of letting Soup rot in a jail cell did not sound unappealing.

"I can't lose me boy," Cudjoe continued. "He rough and he rude, but he me own flesh and blood, and he all I have left in God's world."

He spoke then of his youth, of growing up the son of a fisherman. He had married the daughter of a well-known shipwright. They built a house on a grassy knoll just north of the village, near the Catholic church. For a time, they were happy.

Then their first son, Emmanuel, died in his sleep, at the age of two. "Is a real tragedy, that. We take it hard, the both of us. But we have a next boy, Ignatius, that we call Soup, because he always mixing it up, always dipping a finger in. That is Soup, yes?"

But the mother, he continued, was not right in the head. She wept, frequently and uncontrollably. She began to beat young Soup for the smallest infractions. The violence grew worse with each passing year. "It get so bad, eh-eh. Terrible thing result." He looked me dead in the eye. "There is good reason why the boy so angry."

"No doubt," I said. "You're no longer married?"

Cudjoe lowered his gaze to the floor. "She gone away about the time Soup have twelve years."

A dog barked somewhere off in the depths of the village.

"Where did she go?"

"Away," he said, softly. He set the empty glass on the coffee table. I leaned forward to refill it, but he waved me off.

"I owe Soup me life, is true," Cudjoe said. "He save me, save me in ways I cannot say. It is a debt I will go to me grave to repay."

He stood and nervously adjusted his sleeve. He seemed distraught—frayed, no doubt, by the long day and his mounting worries. I saw him to the door. I assured him that I would consider his proposition, but that I could grant him no assurances. We shook hands, and then he stepped into the blackness of the night.

The boys who raped Edward Jesperson were persuaded to confess and then expelled. The Headmaster announced zero tolerance for "hazing" and suspended, for one semester, recruitment activities for all campus clubs and societies. A pathetic conclusion to an unhappy affair.

Or so I thought.

In fact, it was not concluded: Edward's father filed criminal lawsuits against the boys in question and a civil lawsuit against the Academy for damages resulting from negligent oversight. This was his right, and, it is true, a sort of justice was found. The Academy settled out of court for an undisclosed sum. Three of the offending boys were sentenced to the juvenile hall, their records forever stained.

But if the abuse Edward had suffered at the Academy was terrible, it was the trial that broke him. The exposure of the trial was unmerciful. The boy fell to pieces in that court room; he was beyond shame. And all the while his father sat trembling in a red rage. His could only be a Pyrrhic victory.

It was my great misfortune that the defense strategy included looking into "the culture of the institution." Were all the rules followed equally for all boys at all times? Did each faculty member know the rules, and follow them to the letter?

Such questions are absurd. Education is founded upon the model of the master and the apprentice, the affection the young feel for any teacher passionate about his subject. And every teacher worth his salt attends to his most promising charges accordingly.

In court, I was made to answer a rather awkward series of questions. Yes, over the years, certain boys had been invited into my apartment for tea or a Sunday supper. Such commingling is not wrong, in an official sense. But it is generally frowned upon for a bachelor man to entertain a student privately.

Was liquor served? I am an advocate for responsible drinking. A sip of gin on a hot summer day—after a quick dip at a nearby quarry—never hurt a lad.

And yes, on certain select occasions I had taken a boy to Philadelphia to attend the theatre, or to Washington to visit a museum. It was my pleasure to pay for these excursions. But I am not a rich man, and to share a hotel room—always two beds, mind you—is strictly a financial matter. In any event, the boys who came along did so willingly.

Yes, there are forms that should have been filled out. Yes, the administration should have known where we were.

If I neglected to follow the rules to the letter it was sheer negligence, not some insidious attempt to corrupt a charge.

Ask any of my boys: I never once touched them. Not once.

Obviously, none of this had any direct relevance to the charges being adjudicated. None of the accused had ever been in my private company. Nor had Edward Jesperson. Yet there they were, one after the other, my best boys, called by the defense: Thomas Goodman, Jeremiah Pappas, Philip Chadwick. Clearly, they had been coached by the defense; clearly, the questions were carefully phrased so as to imply far more than they literally stated.

In the end, as I say, this proved to be a most unproductive line of inquiry and a waste of everyone's time. The accused were all found guilty. After all, they were criminals! Rapists! For young Edward Jesperson, the trial ended. But for at least one innocent bystander, me, a person whose only mistake had been to act out of pity and compassion, there was more.

In an exhibition of good taste for which I shall always be grateful, the Academy invited me to apply for a sabbatical, despite the fact that I was not technically eligible. I had just won a small prize for my first book, *Molluscan Species of the North Atlantic*. On the strength of that project, my publisher had commissioned a glossy, travel-oriented collection on Caribbean seashells—a rare opportunity to break into a new market. Book contract in hand, I was rewarded by the Academy with a six-month paid leave. I did not waste time but immediately booked passage to Carriacou (on the recommendation of my publisher).

The rules governing my return to the Academy were strict. It was a dignified and just agreement, one which called for a lengthy and, I felt, eloquent letter of resignation.

My references from the Academy were first rate. When I did return to the States, some two years later, I had little trouble establishing myself at a co-ed preparatory school in northern Arizona, where I worked until my recent retirement.

Two days after receiving Cudjoe's request for assistance, I left on a scheduled trip to Fort-de-France, Martinique, and its Museum of Natural Science. In the mornings, I pored over their extensive shell collection and consulted with the staff. Each afternoon, after a light lunch and a cappuccino, I bought a copy of the *International Herald Tribune* and read it in La Place de la Savanne, a large park fragrant with roses and salt air. Across the common stood the public library, with its fantastic gold dome and massive pillars, the very definition of stately colonial eminence. Evenings found me wandering the cobblestone streets, stopping in at whatever bistro caught my eye. It was a pleasant week, during which I felt blissfully anonymous, neither beholden nor responsible to any man. Perfectly free, perfectly alone.

Yet I thought frequently of my friend, Cudjoe. I feared not for Soup—let the little despot meet his fate. But for his father, I was torn. I weighed the merits of the case. Couldn't I at least visit with Leopold Roberts and ask him what he intended to accomplish? But the thought of sitting even for five minutes in that lawyer's office, smelling his body odor and suffering his bombastic oratory, repulsed me. Were there not other, more competent lawyers in Grenada? Surely I could visit one in the capital, on my return to the island. The very thought of such a first step made my head swim. No, I thought, do not offer assistance unless you intend to follow up on it. Your friend deserves a clear, honest response.

Yet the matter seemed anything but clear.

I had, you now understand, absolutely no desire to come within reach of a lawyer or a courtroom. Even if I were to cooperate from behind the scenes, there were certain issues to consider, not the least of them the question of setting a precedent. To many West Indians, a white foreigner means one thing: money. Take a stroll along the Carenage in St. George's, if you doubt me. Try to pass through the market unnoticed and unheeded.

You will be solicited unceasingly, and without mercy. You will be yelled at, called to, grabbed, groped, pressed and poked. Perhaps worse. No, to be a white man in the West Indies is to be a mark, and caution is the order of the day.

This is not to say that I felt Cudjoe was trying to take advantage of me. I knew his need was great, and I knew his request was serious and substantial. But to come to his assistance would surely send a message to his fellow villagers, and who knows what might follow? A bevy of supplicants, I feared.

In hindsight, I have often told myself that I should have heeded this practical argument, I should have drawn a clear line and held it. But I did not. I wavered, and for the simple reason that my motives, my interests, were anything but clear.

My truest motive—I must confess!—was anything but altruistic; I still desired Soup to acknowledge me, if not apologize. I wanted him to speak my name and to call me . . . if not a friend, then an ally. A brother.

The excitement of this pursuit, as I thought upon it, was intense. I understood that, on some level, I had a certain kind of rare opportunity. For Soup, the poor fool, had cornered himself. The precious tightness of our encounter might, I thought, engender new opportunities. In my final, mad hour of fantasy, the point became not in the least what to make of Soup's dilemma, but only, very delightfully and very damnably, where to put one's hand on it.

Her Majesty's Prison sits atop a steep hill overlooking St. George's. From the waiting room I studied the quilt of rusting tin roofs nestled alongside the dignified, russet-colored tiles of Parliament House and the Anglican cathedral, and, on the point, Fort George, colonial sentinel, its sturdy gray stone a timeless reminder of the island's rich and complicated past. In the harbor, a blue and white banana freighter sat alongside the fruits warehouse. Workers, with their guy lines and longshoreman's poles, maneuvered pallet after pallet of fruit packed in cardboard boxes. And so the island's meager economy spurted along, box by box.

Arranging an audience required some diligence—that is, a few crisp bills placed in the right hands.

Shortly after two, Soup was brought before me. The rough-hewn stone walls of the visitation room were peppered with patches of moss and black mold. The wind whistled through the jalousies (reinforced with iron bars, but of course). Soup, handsome in his tight-fitting white shirt and pants, refused to look me in the eye.

I told him that his father had requested my assistance, but before I committed myself, I wanted to know: Did he, too, wish for my help? What might we, together, hope to accomplish? Was he willing, for instance, to plead guilty to a lesser offense—obstructing government business—if it meant we might be able to quietly dismiss the assault charge?

The boy was rude. He exhibited no interest in my plan whatsoever. He demonstrated not one iota of gratitude. He answered no questions, even when I stressed that I needed some positive sign from him before I could proceed. Couldn't he at least nod?

In a moment of desperation, I held forth my hand and asked only that he hold it. That touch would be, I assured him, a beginning.

"Please," I said, "let me call you friend."

He spat in my palm.

"Very well," I said, wiping my hand on my trousers. "I'll take that as a refusal."

Muttering a patois curse, Soup rose from his chair and called for the guard. Within a half-minute he was gone from my sight, without so much as a word for his father.

I ordered a taxi to deliver me posthaste to the Radisson in Grand Anse. At the beachside bar, I all but dove into the first of several Beefeater Gibsons. I spoke the Queen's English with a cluster of vacationing Brits. They were positively charming on the topic of football, but less so when the discussion turned to John Major's social policies. What can an American say of British politics? We're ignorant as dogs.

The next morning, I woke to the rhythmic singing of Cudjoe's cutlass as he tended to the grass in Dutchie's yard. I rose and took a cup of coffee out onto my porch. Seeing me, Cudjoe straightened. I called out a greeting. He inquired of my trip to Martinique, and I told him that I had enjoyed it greatly. We spoke of that day's weather: steel-gray thunderheads loomed on the eastern horizon, obscuring the early sun and promising a late morning shower. A copper-colored dinghy bobbed in the choppy surf of the bay: a fisherman collecting his morning catch, or perhaps securing his fish pots in advance of the coming storm.

"Your son . . . ," I began. But I knew not how to continue. I found myself wholly unprepared to discuss the matter of my ill-fated trip to St. George's.

"I still waiting and hoping, sir." He took a kerchief from his pocket and daubed his brow.

I allowed myself to be distracted by a bus rolling past on the road. I needlessly waved to it; the driver beeped his horn in polite response. When I turned back to Cudjoe, I found he'd resumed his work. Ashamed, I took my coffee inside and quietly shut my door.

It rained for the next ten days, a Biblical downpour that soaked the island without respite, sky and sea one slate-colored mass. The dirt roads became soft clay beds, riven with streams and puddles; pastures become sodden bogs. No shepherds ambled through the fields behind my house, singing their songs; no school children clustered at the foot of my lane, waiting for the bus, laughing and playing the fool. And, of course, Cudjoe did not attend to Dutchie's grounds. In Grenada, when it rains like that, all outdoor labor ceases.

One afternoon, desperate for a brick of cheese and a splash of rum, I pulled on my Wellingtons and a rain parka and set out for a smaller shop in the village. One would have thought the Black Plague had struck. Every street and lane and path, every bench and shop corner and half-wall—all the places ordinarily populated by the villagers on their rounds: empty. Indeed, the only people I found were the two soldiers assigned guard duty out front of Dutchie's shop. Thin streams of water cascaded from their plastic ponchos. Out of pity, I waved to them. No response.

Holed up in my bungalow, I worked long and hard. I had a great number of shells to clean and polish in preparation for a photo shoot in Trinidad, and while work has always been a solace, it could not wholly ameliorate my growing sense of isolation. For I had come to care for and depend upon the amiable chitchat of the men in the village square, the bantering of the market women, or the friendly toot of a bus driver's horn. These villagers all knew me by name, greeted me with a smile. They'd all but accepted me as one of their own. Denied these small graces, I was confronted with the unpleasant fact of my own isolation and loneliness: a middle-aged expatriate scraping clean seashells and listening to French shortwave radio. Cudjoe, the person closest to me on this tiny island—why had I turned away?

I knew then that I must cross that distance.

A few days later, the rain miraculously ceased and, instantaneously, the island bounced back to life. I spent a pleasant afternoon in the village, shopping and waving to everyone that I saw, stopping to chat with shop owners and the men in the village square. Everyone spoke of the rain, of the mudslides north of the village, of the washed-out roads. Everyone was thankful that cisterns and rain barrels were brimming with fresh water. On that happy day, I felt a special closeness to these people; I felt welcome among them, a part of the scene.

I resolved, on that very day, to find my friend Cudjoe and to speak my piece before him. This would best be accomplished with some kind of token of my appreciation for his presence in my life. I spent the afternoon in my kitchen, preparing a jolly meal. When it was complete, I wrapped a platter of food in foil and set out to find my friend's house.

It took some doing. I wandered about the nether regions of the village, asking many for directions. Always, I received a vague wave of a hand and the assurance that Cudjoe's residence was "just there" or "over so." Ultimately, this proved to be a clapboard house perched atop an isolated knoll. It was near dusk when I stepped into his yard. My friend sat astride a tree stump, wearing only a pair of worn canvas shorts. Between his legs was a fish trap he was wrapping in chicken wire. He stood as I approached and pulled on a sun-bleached T-shirt.

"I brought you something," I said, proffering the platter of food.

He grinned. "Is what we cooking tonight, sir?"

I pulled back the foil. I had attempted a goat curry stew, with pigeon peas, brown rice, and, of course, boiled callaloo. Cudjoe burst out laughing; it made my heart glad to hear him so joyful. With a sharp whistle, he called out to a young girl, perhaps just nine or ten, in the yard next door. He introduced her as his grand-niece, and immediately sent her down the trace with instructions to return with a bottle of rum on trust from Mr. Richie's shop.

Cudjoe ate with genuine relish, and was so good as to compliment me on the robust curry and on the moistness of the rice. "I doesn't like dry rice," he said. "You cooking a good meal, Mr. Carter."

His grand-niece soon returned with the rum, and then began a long night of drinking, very uncustomary for the both of us. Cudjoe seemed genuinely happy to have me there, and eager to talk. It was I who broached the subject of his son. Had he heard anything from him?

"Not a thing," he muttered. "To get a word from the prison—it ain't easy, Mr. Carter. Many crosses to bear, sir. Many crosses to bear. I fear something happen to the boy. He in danger, real danger. Them prison guards, eh-eh. All of them dogheart straight through."

"I'm sorry, what's that?"

"To have dogheart," he said, "is to be cold and cruel for so. Is to put a man under heavy manners, yes." He drew his shirtsleeve across his mouth, slowly. "Mr. Carter, sir, forgive. But I must ask just one more time. Could you see your way, sir?"

Smiling, I picked up the bottle of rum. "Precisely the matter I have come to discuss with you, Cudjoe." I tilted the bottle forward; Cudjoe held his glass out and I poured us each another finger of rum. "You know that I am a teacher in my own country."

Yes, he said, he knew that. "You a very important man, Mr. Carter. Important in truth."

"You're very kind to say so." We raised our glasses and toasted one another. "Lately, Cudjoe, I have been thinking quite a lot about my boys." And I explained how, when I first arrived in Carriacou, I was glad to be away from the Academy. I passed a pleasant summer with nary a thought of what I'd left behind. Yet, with the onset of autumn came the sight of local children padding off to school, the girls in their billowy skirts and clean blouses, the lads looking smart in their starched white shirts and pressed trousers. Each morning I sat on my porch with a cup of coffee, watching the boys at the foot of the lane as they waited for the morning bus: their lean, hard limbs, their playful antics, their satchels bulging with books and materials.

Naturally, my thoughts turned to my own boys. I missed their orderly procession into chapel on Sunday morning, so handsome in their navy blazers and school ties. I missed the tink of bats meeting balls on the playing fields outside my office window, the cheers from the dugout, the smell of fresh grass on a spring breeze. I missed the older boys who loitered about the lab after class; they had learned to love science, and they loved it because of me, through me. With me. I missed the youngest boys, the new arrivals, scared and intimidated by the upperclassmen. Most of all, I missed the lonely boys, shipped off by disinterested parents. Soon enough they would grow their tough exteriors, but before they were protected by these shells, they sometimes came to me. Weeping. Terrorized.

I took a long swallow of rum, bracing myself for what I had planned next to say. "One student," I said, "Edward Jesperson . . ."

"Yes," said Cudjoe.

"Understand," I said, my voice shaking, "I saw something of myself in him. He was so alone. I know what it is to be alone. My mother died when I was two. I always thought her loss should have drawn me closer to my father. But I'm afraid the opposite was true. He provided the funds for my education, for my material comfort. But it did not extend beyond that. I always hoped that he would find a way to include me in his world. But he never did."

I turned the empty glass against the inside of my palm. We sat quietly for a long minute. My father had been dead for a decade. I was dismayed to find the anger and the bitterness still so close.

Finally, Cudjoe let out a long sigh. "To be a father is the most difficult thing. Children a blessing and a burden both, you know. Don't be so quick to judge a man. It ain't easy, Mr. Carter, it ain't easy."

"All that rum," I said, shaking my head. "I meant to speak to you of Edward Jesperson."

Cudjoe turned to me. "Mr. Carter, forgive the impertinence. It is funny, eh? You talk to make a living. Always, you know what you want to say. You want to say something to me about my son, about Soup. But what you want to say is not always what you need to say. Tonight you say what you need to say, despite yourself."

There are few times, goodness knows, when I, Gerald Prescott Carter, am at a loss for words. That moment was one. Cudjoe's comment unnerved me; I can't say just why. It was all I could do to muster the strength to stand. I asked my host to excuse me, and walked around the corner of the house to relieve myself against the side of the hill.

When I returned to the yard, Cudjoe had collected the glasses and the bottle and stored them away. He stood in the dark of the clearing, polishing my platter with a cloth, his strokes slow and firm.

"I'll have another drink of rum," I announced.

"You will not."

I threw my shoulders back, preparing to speak. But Cudjoe just shook his head. "Come, I walk you down the hill."

"Thank you, but I know the way."

He handed me my platter. "As you like."

I took several steps into the darkness. Then I turned and faced my friend. "You have asked me to come to the aid of your son," I said. "I saw him in prison, in St. George's. He doesn't want my help. Your son is very angry. And impossibly rude. I'm sorry, Cudjoe, but I cannot help a man who does not desire my assistance."

Cudjoe's eyes narrowed, and he lifted his chin. He seemed to regard me from a very great distance. "Father must forgive the son, Mr. Carter. Just as son must one day forgive the father."

I had the good sense and dignity to leave without opening my mouth to speak.

It was the third week in November when the screw took its final turn. Cornelius Cudjoe began a protest in front of Dutchie's store. Sitting with his legs crossed and back erect, his cutlass before him, he read from a worn copy of the Holy Bible in a lilting, rhythmic voice. Paul's Letters to the Corinthians: a plea for faith, hope, love, and forgiveness.

I had come into the village for supplies and was shocked to see him like this. When he set down the book to sip water from a glass jar, I stepped forward and, with a placating grin directed toward the soldiers still posted outside Dutchie's door, knelt beside my friend. He did not turn his gaze from the front door of Dutchie's shop. I asked him what in the world he was doing there.

"Cudjoe not moving until Soup release. The matter in Dutchie's hands now. I waiting for him to come to terms with the Customs fellow."

I told Cudjoe that I was worried for him. When the patience of the soldiers wore thin, they might forcibly remove him. I pointed to his cutlass. "Tell me you won't fight anyone."

"A working man does travel with he cutlass, Mr. Carter. But Cudjoe ain't come to fight. I come to force a solution for me boy. Dutchie get me boy into this thing, and Dutchie going to get him out."

"Cudjoe, I doubt a few readings from the Holy Bible will accomplish much."

"Is hunger strike," he responded, straightening his spine. "No food until Soup release."

From his stern, resolute demeanor I gathered that he actually believed his plan might work. "Come to your senses, man. This is absurd."

He turned to face me. "What other option Cudjoe have?"

I must admit, the words stung. And, as I did not have a response, I left him there, sitting in the dirt. He shortly returned to his recitations.

I could not work that day for worry. That night I slept but little. At dawn, I rose and walked back to the village square. Cudjoe had not moved. A plate of baked fish with a portion of rice and pigeon peas sat on the dusty ground beside his cutlass. Flies hopped about it. Was the plate left out of generosity or spite? Out of compassion or ridicule? I could not tell. I refilled Cudjoe's water jar. I begged him to quit. But he would not speak to me. Not even a shake of the head. He just kept reading his Bible, his voice now cracked and rough, his delivery a flat monotone, devoid of conviction.

I spent a second day fidgeting and fussing about my bungalow, unable to concentrate. At dusk, a glass of gin perspiring in my hand, I tuned the shortwave to a French station and stepped onto my porch. A fisherman passed along the shoreside road, home from his long day at sea.

"Is Cudjoe still sitting in the square?" I called.

"Yes, man," he returned, "the damn fool stubborn for so!"

One of Dutchie's curs broke from under the house, running along the cyclone fence, barking at the fisherman. Without breaking stride, the fisherman reached into his croker sack and extracted a silvery jackfish and tossed it over the fence. The dog ate its meal in two snaps, tail wagging excitedly. On the radio, François Hardy crooned *"Comment te dire adieu?"*

"Tell me why you have come here, friend," Dutchie said. We sat in his living room, filled with overstuffed leather furniture and stout, teak tables. A white shag rug covered the tile floor. He had poured me a glass of Johnnie Walker Black Label, considered the classiest drink on the island.

I told him I was there to make an appeal for the Cudjoes, both son and father.

Dutchie took a long drag on his cigar, expelling a thick cloud of smoke between us. He was a short man with skin the color of cocoa butter, and sported a thick, black beard. He wore his white shirt half-unbuttoned, the better to display his gold necklaces.

"The matter is out of my hands."

"Surely it is not," I returned. "A man in your position? I have to think there are strings that might be pulled." When he showed no sign of interest, I added, "A man's life is at stake."

Dutchie laughed. "How well do you know Cornelius Cudjoe?"

"We are friends," I said. "There is no one closer to me on this island."

"You know he was married once?"

"Yes. His wife left him, or was sent away."

"No, she is dead." Dutchie reached over and tapped the ash from his cigar. "You have seen Cudjoe's scar?" He slowly drew a finger from behind his ear, down along the neck. I nodded. "That was the first time that the woman tried to kill him. She very nearly succeeded. He should have left her then. We all knew she would try again."

I sat forward. "What happened?"

"No one is quite certain. Some say the woman rushed Cudjoe a second time and he was forced to defend himself. Others suspect she went after Soup. Cudjoe may have pushed her down. Her death may have been accidental. But many think otherwise."

"Are you saying that Cudjoe killed his wife?"

He shrugged. What police found that morning, he said, was a woman in the yard with the back of her head split open. A stone, a tire iron—something heavy had been used, though no weapon was ever found. There was no witness. Just a husband sitting beneath a mango tree, weeping. "To this day," Dutchie said, "Cudjoe has never spoken of what he did. Or saw."

I sat back in my chair, flabbergasted. Cornelius Cudjoe could never lay a hand on anyone in violence, of this I was sure. "And Soup?" I asked. "Did he witness this?"

"The boy claimed to have been tending sheep that morning."

"So was it ruled a murder or an accident?"

"Officially, it was overlooked. You see, your friend Cudjoe found an ally in history. This took place in 1983, the year that your country invaded mine. The transition from the Communist government to the puppet democracy of Nicholas Brathwaite was . . . uneven. Many crimes were overlooked." Dutchie chuckled. "Many criminals walk among us, still."

"Surely no one thinks Cudjoe murdered his wife deliberately," I said. "It was self-defense, if anything."

"The village has a long memory, and its own way of passing judgment, rightly or wrongly. That is why Cudjoe's protest is so pathetic. No one will stand with him, even if he is right. Which he is not."

"So why would you hire the Cudjoes," I asked, "if the rest of the village shuns them?"

"They are family," Dutchie replied. "Cudjoe is a cousin to my mother. And both are strong workers, silent and dependable. I value that. Would you like another drink?"

I declined, for Scotch has always made my stomach uneasy.

"You see," Dutchie continued, "I am not concerned with ancient questions about who did what. But I have limits. When Soup was arrested for interfering with the Customs agent, that was one thing. But to strike a police officer? No, I am sorry. The boy is digging his own trench now." He tapped the ash from his cigar. "You know, they say he never shed one tear for his mother? He didn't even attend the funeral. The boy is strange, eh?"

I acknowledged that Soup might be hard to help. But, surely, Dutchie could do something for the father? "A token gesture, even a small effort, might dissuade him from this hunger strike. He is just thick-headed enough to persist until he does himself harm."

Dutchie shook his head. "I'm a bit busy just now. I have no time for petty affairs. And you, Mr. Carter, should enjoy our nice, quiet island. Enjoy the beaches and sailing. Enjoy a glass of rum. But you should not draw undue attention to a matter of private business. That would be most unwelcome."

Smoothing the crease on my trousers, I sat forward in my chair. "Yes, of course, but surely—"

Dutchie held up his hand, his fingers stiff and erect. At the base of that thick, stout hand was a curious tattoo, some kind of visage, or mask. The angry eyes blazed with rage, the mouth a tight, grim frown. A death mask, I wondered, or the face of a vengeful god? Regardless, it frightened me terribly.

I removed a handkerchief from my pocket and daubed at my forehead. I was suddenly quite warm, my sweat glands pumping and pulse racing. Soon, I would need my milk of magnesia and an aspirin. I wasted no more time with Dutchie. Placing my empty glass on the marble-topped table, I assured him that his message had been received.

"Very good." He stood from his chair and bid me good night, then disappeared into the dark recesses of his house. The night watchman showed me to the gate, which he closed behind me with a great rattling of chains and the snap of a bolt lock.

I sat long on my porch that night. Moonlight danced on the sea, a glittering road from some fairy tale leading, invariably, to some sad end. Had Cornelius Cudjoe killed his wife? It seemed impossible. He was a kind and gentle man, infinitely patient. I could not imagine him raising his hand against anyone. What, then, could I imagine? I had but fragments of the story. I could only speculate—which I did, freely. For this was the story that I needed to know.

I took as my premise that Cudjoe had not killed his wife, not even in self-defense. That left only one plausible hypothesis: Soup had committed matricide not out of spite, but to protect his father. For the husband refused to lift a hand against the wife, regardless of the danger. And there had been danger on that morning. Soup had seen it before; he'd seen his mother slash his father's neck, nearly killing him. His father's reaction—not anger or hatred, but love and mercy, forgiveness and understanding—made little sense to a boy who'd grown up with a mother like his: indifferent when she wasn't outright cruel, beating him for the smallest thing. For nothing. She went after the father, too, throwing rocks and cooking pans and crying out that Cudjoe had murdered their first son. When she was like that, she had to be watched. But his father seemed blind, willing to live with the woman because, he said, it was his solemn responsibility.

Soup could never understand his father. His young mind irreversibly scarred, he'd learned to hit back, to defend himself against all comers. You didn't stop to ask why someone was after you; their reasons were never sensible. You simply fought for yourself. On that bright morning, as he readied himself to go into the pastures to tend sheep, Soup watched his mother, cutlass in hand, chopping kindling for the cook fire and eyeing his father, who sat in the corner of the yard, his back to the house, mending a net. The mother stood from her small pile of faggots. She stepped quietly, slowly across the dirt yard, cutlass in hand. She lifted the bright blade. Soup sprang from behind the house, sharp stone in hand . . .

Cudjoe only turned when he heard a cutlass rattle against the stones in the yard. Then, the manic rustling in the bushes—an animal in flight. His wife sprawled awkwardly in the yard, blood blackening the dirt. One hand twitched against the pocket of her apron, dusty with baking flour.

So began a period of unspeakable grief and mourning. The aftermath of the murder could only have been a black blur of pain and confusion. Coming out of that, surfacing back into the world of the village, was not easy. The death of his wife did not end Cudjoe's troubles, but rather compounded them. Cudjoe silently shouldered the blame for the incident, suffering the condemnation of his fellow villagers, who might understand the crime but could never forgive it—unless he were to confess the truth. Which he did not, for a father could never hand over a son for judgment. He would never speak a word of what he knew. And, once he understood that no authority would pursue the case, he realized that he did not need to speak of it. Silence became a form of protection for his son.

Red-eyed and infirm, I stumbled into the village square at dawn, intent on sharing my inferences with Cudjoe. The time had come, I felt, for him to share his story. But he was nowhere to be found.

I soon heard the sad news: Soup had been killed in St. George's. Some said he'd been jumped by fellow inmates; others that he'd been beaten by the guards. It was impossible to get the details straight. In any case, he was dead.

I was one of the few villagers to attend the funeral. Whatever old grudges, whatever false judgments had been passed, it seemed that nothing had been forgiven or forgotten in this, Cudjoe's blackest hour. Of course, I wanted to speak with my friend, to share with him what I had surmised. But the period of mourning was not the appropriate time. And, in any event, Cudjoe left the island the next day to visit relatives in St. Lucia.

Within a week, the Customs matter cleared itself up as mysteriously as it had begun. Dutchie's store reopened and the villagers resumed shopping there. The weekend hordes of mainlanders and tourists soon descended again, buying up the contraband televisions and liquor. Out of convenience and, yes, out of frugality, I too resumed shopping there, though it would always be with some measure of distaste.

My book project was progressing rapidly, and I spent January moving between Port-of-Spain, Kingston, and Fort-de-France, finalizing my research and photographing hundreds of specimens. In early February, I returned to Carriacou, where I intended to start my first draft. (The first of many subsequent editorial deadlines loomed.) I made a point of stopping by Cudjoe's house but found it boarded shut and locked. Still in St. Lucia, I imagined, visiting relatives. So I made my way to the village square, where I loitered on the benches beneath the palm trees, sipping a cold beer as I caught up on the gossip.

It was there I learned that, on a morning in late January, Cudjoe had emerged, naked, from the sea grape along the shore just beneath the Catholic church. Ignoring both the laughter and the ribald greetings of the fishermen stocking their dinghies for a morning's work, Cudjoe had walked into the water and started swimming. The men paid him little mind, though Cudjoe was not known to be a swimmer. But as he moved out farther into the bay, the men realized that he was not aimed for the sandy shoals that shadow one part of the reef—a popular swimming destination—but for the narrow break that gave unto the open waters of the Caribbean.

The tide was going out that morning, and he felt borne along by its gentle pull. The sea beckoned to him, singing, soft susurrus of sound. Waves plashed and stroked him, lifted and lowered him, buffeted and rolled him. As he swam, he felt himself washed clean. The heavy darkness began to lift itself from his spirit. With each stroke he felt closer to that thing he longed for, but could not precisely name.

By the time he made the reef, he could hear the humming engines and the shouts of the men coming after him. He swam past the yellow plastic crate lashed tightly to a pole that served as a makeshift buoy.

Colder, stronger water swirled around him.

Raising a hand against the wind, fingers splayed, he spoke a name, once. Then he slipped beneath the final wave, swallowing the sea.

About the Author

Rob Davidson was born in 1967 in Duluth, Minnesota, and was educated at Beloit College and Purdue University. From 1990-92, he served with the U. S. Peace Corps in the Eastern Caribbean, where he taught high school English language and literature. He is the author of *Field Observations: Stories* (University of Missouri Press, 2001) and *The Master and the Dean: The Literary Criticism of Henry James and William Dean Howells* (University of Missouri Press, 2005). His awards and honors include winning the 2009 Camber Press Fiction Award, judged by Ron Carlson; a 1997 AWP Intro Journals Project Award; a Pushcart Prize nomination; and having twice been selected Artist-in-Residence at the Byrdcliffe Arts Colony in Woodstock, New York. Davidson's fiction, essays and interviews have appeared in *ZYZZYVA, Hayden's Ferry Review, Indiana Review, The Normal School, New Delta Review,* and elsewhere. Davidson teaches creative writing and American literature at California State University, Chico.